Ellis Peters has gained universal acclaim for her crime novels, and in particular for *The Chronicles of Brother Cadfael*, now into their seventeenth volume.

Death Mask

Ellis Peters

HEADLINE

ISBN 0 7472 3372 1

Printed and bound in Great Britain by
HarperCollins Manufacturing, Glasgow

HEADLINE BOOK PUBLISHING
A division of Hodder Headline PLC
338 Euston Road
London NW1 3BH

CHAPTER I

I WAS WANDERING moodily down a street in Bloomsbury, fingering the loose silver in my trouser pocket, which represented all the ready cash I had between myself and Aunt Caroline's spare room, and wondering whether the old girl would find it worth a loan not to have me on the premises, when some hall or other suddenly began to disgorge its audience across my path at the end of some lecture or other, and there among the bald heads and the quivering beards and the earnest, dowdy students was this totally improbable woman.

I stopped in my tracks for the pleasure of watching her walk. Just of watching her walk, that's all. She sailed out of the doorway and down the steps, her shoulders well back, her head afloat like a flower on its stem; and her gaze seemed to be fixed always a little above everything that crossed her path, as though her sights were raised for a longer journey than the one which was apparent. Everything she did would always carry that implication of another, less obvious, significance hidden somewhere behind and beyond the act as other people saw it.

Her clothes were the last word in sophistication; so austere that virtually there was nothing there but a slender casing of two or three luxurious materials, and the shape of the body within them. And, of course, the hat, which was an enormous flat grey tam-o'-shanter in what I suppose was probably some kind of nylon tulle. She wore it not straight, which was the mode, to judge by what I'd seen around me in those few hours in London, but tilted slightly forward towards her brows, which prevented me from getting a clear view of her face; but all the rest of her would have been more at home at a modiste's cocktail party, or Ascot, or a smart first night, than a few hundred yards from the British Museum, listening to a lecture on—I stepped back to take another look at the announcement at the foot of the steps—" New Light on the Origins of Mycenæan Culture," by Professor J. Barclay.

I stood back against the wall, and watched her. I wasn't the only one thus occupied, and no wonder. Even some of the grey heads turned, some of the didactic conversations lapsed into yearning silences, as she came slowly down the steps, and stood hesitating for a moment, irresolutely fingering the strap of her handbag on her gloved wrist, and re-adjusting the book under her arm. Her movements had a certain curious sadness. First she had moved impetuously, now she halted and wavered, took a few quick steps, and then looked back towards the doorway of the hall. She was not meant for irresolution ; you felt that for her to hesitate was to suffer.

I had nowhere particular to go, and there was no hurry about getting there ; I hadn't even much to think about, except where I was going to spend the night, and how I was going to get another job at short notice, and for the moment I wasn't even deeply interested in either of those problems. I much preferred to stand quietly in the darkness, watching this woman, and speculating idly about her. Why should she be in need of new light on the origins of Mycenæan culture? Was she, by some freakish chance, as intelligent and intellectually inclined as she was beautiful and elegant ? Or had she taken cover here from a date she wanted to avoid ? Or was she, perhaps, only the dutiful spouse of Professor J. Barclay, obliged by her sense of loyalty to put in an appearance at his lecture ? Queerer things than that happened where women were concerned. But in that case why should she hover outside the hall afterwards ? She'd be inside helping him to acknowledge the congratulations of his admirers, and fend off the shafts of his rivals. What, in any case, was she waiting for ? The audience was already dispersing in a murmur of erudite conversation into the streets of Bloomsbury. Only the last few lingered on the pavement to finish mild disputes and gossip over their good nights.

People do, of course, have their own, usually blameless, reasons for hanging about in the streets, in darkness and silence, apparently waiting, in that curiously evocative, even ominous manner which makes one approach them with sudden trepidation, aware that one's life may be about to ricochet from this momentary contact, and go off at an unforeseen and disconcerting tangent. Take, for instance, that long, motionless shadow in the heavily shadowed doorway across the street, some twenty yards away to my right. But for one slight movement as a car passed by I shouldn't have known there was a man there at all. Waiting as tranquil, as withdrawn as that opened an endless prospect for speculation.

To be honest, my life was badly in need of a new direction ; but I was no longer young enough to feel great pleasure in the processes of change.

A tall, erect, middle-aged man strode out of the doorway of the hall, called a good night over his shoulder, and descended the steps. Professor J. Barclay ? General Barclay one might rather have labelled him on his appearance. I caught a glimpse of a clipped moustache, high and prominent cheek-bones, a large forehead, thick, grizzled brows. He didn't cross to one of the parked cars across the street, nor halt to look round for a cruising taxi, but swung left at the foot of the steps, and walked briskly away. Nor did the woman make any move to intercept him. She had looked up at him quickly as he emerged from the doorway, and seemed inclined for a moment to step forward ; and then, instead, she stepped back, into the shadows, with a movement of resignation, and a turn of her head that was like a sigh. He passed by her without a glance.

The woman had decided to leave, too. She turned slowly in my direction ; and as she did so the shadows shifted in the doorway on the other side of the street, and the motionless watcher stepped out and began to walk towards us. Everything seemed charged with significance, as though I were being handed the three disconnected clues for a treasure hunt. The door of the house had not opened ; there had been no light. He had simply stepped out of the darkness and begun to walk along the street, not hurriedly, not stealthily, keeping a long, even stride. He was very tall, and lean within his light overcoat. Now he was crossing the street ; in a matter of seconds he would be passing the spot where I stood. And within a few yards of me, one way or the other, he would meet the woman.

She lifted her head, and for the first time I caught a glimpse of her face, and I realised with a stab of still painful recollection how like Dorothy she was. Then the light of the street lamp fell full upon her, and I saw that it was Dorothy.

I hadn't set eyes on her for over seventeen years, not since the day I asked her to marry me and she turned me down. And there wasn't much external resemblance between this remarkably elegant woman of—let's see, it must be thirty-five !—and that wild young creature of eighteen, elegant, too, in a lawless way, like an unbroken greyhound. Her brows were still high, shapely, and unplucked, and still gave her that faintly bewildered look of her extreme youth, as though the world never failed to astonish her. The poise of the hat and the poise of the head combined to detach her a little farther from the object of her wonder, as though she drew back to take a measured view, but without ridding herself of the impulse of startled disbelief.

And of course, I thought, enjoying the glimpse of her

more than I'd dreamed possible, she won't know me from
Adam by this time; and even if she did, she wouldn't
particularly want to meet me again. Why should she? We
can hardly have much to say to each other, after seventeen
years.

" Evelyn ! " cried Dorothy, in her high, unself-conscious
voice, calling half Bloomsbury to bear witness to her surprise and delight; and she bore down on me with the old
imperious stride, her hands out and reaching for mine. The
book fell from under her arm, and splayed its pages on the
moist pavement.

Two of us reached for it at the same instant. The tall,
thin man had checked in mid-stride; a long, lean hand was
outstretched close to mine, a corded wrist, seamed with a
short, wrinkled scar, shot out from the sleeve of the light
overcoat. I looked up at close quarters into a craggy face,
split in two by a hawk's beak of a nose. Black, narrowed
eyes, set in weathered, leathery sockets, looked back at me
impenetrably. He smiled very slightly, withdrew courteously,
and looked beyond me to Dorothy with a long, long, intent
stare before he turned and walked on, to disappear into the
darkness.

And I forgot him before he vanished. What else was I
likely to do, standing there face to face with Dorothy?

" Evelyn! I thought you were thousands of miles away,
in the Persian Gulf, or somewhere. How lovely to see you
again ! Why haven't you ever written? Are you still angry
with me ? "

Very few women but Dorothy, I suppose, would greet a
man with that question after seventeen years, just because
on the last occasion when they met him they happened to
turn down his offer of marriage. And probably no one but
Dorothy could approach him with the assumption that he
would still be angry about it, and be dead right.

" Don't be an ass ! " I said, which, besides not being at

all what I'd meant to say, was also a prevarication, if not a downright lie. I *was* still sore about that refusal. I hadn't realised it until I saw her again. Seventeen years blew away like a scud of dead leaves in the wind. " When did we ever write letters to each other ? How are you, Dorothy ? You're looking wonderful."

" I wasn't feeling wonderful," she said, " until now. Evelyn, are you really not angry ? You do *look* cross. Are you sure it's not with me ? "

" It's not with you," I assured her. " There's nobody in the world I could be more glad to see."

She tilted her head back to look at me long and earnestly from under the shadow of the enormous hat, and I caught the full glow of those great eyes of hers, dark as violets, and saw the long, pure, slanting line of her cheek-bones. She had always the air of an extremely aristocratic model, except that her eyes and mouth were kind, and wild, and alive in the patrician face, instead of fashionably blank. " Don't just go away from me with only a few polite words, I want to know all about you. Give me this evening ! Unless, of course, you've got a date already ? "

" I've only been back in London three hours," I said, " and I haven't seen a soul I know yet, apart from the firm." I mopped the faint, moist stains from her book, and offered it to her, and she took it as though she'd never seen it before, shrugged a little, and tucked it under her arm.

" Actually I didn't understand a word of it, you have to learn the language first. Bruce was easy enough to follow, but then, Bruce was hardly what one would call an expert —and this man is *the* expert. How long are you going to be in England, Evelyn ? You're on leave, I suppose ? "

" Not leave—I'm out on my ear."

" Evelyn ! " she gasped, staring up at me in consternation. " They couldn't be so ungrateful ! After all you've done for the company——"

" The company's out on its ear too. Hadn't you heard ? The local oil industry is now a native affair. We've all got the push."

" But how idiotic ! The Sultanate will lose all its income——"

" It isn't a Sultanate any longer. They've had a revolution. Not before it was time ! "

" How awful for you ! " she said. " I'm so sorry ! Then you're out of a job ? Absolutely free ? "

It sounded like the kind of freedom I might be in a hurry to surrender, but I didn't bother to say so. " Don't be sorry ! I'd had enough, I was glad to come home. And the Sultan was no loss to anyone. He'll do far less harm on the Riviera, and help the local trade no end. He was no good for anything at home."

" But the company will find you another job, of course ? " Was I dreaming, or did I detect a note of discouragement in her tone ?

" The company doesn't see its way. Times are bad. They're paying us off with a month's salary in compensation." I didn't tell her I'd lost my temper and told the personnel manager what the directors could do with their month's salary, and walked out without accepting it. That's the sort of thing you regret afterwards, when you begin counting your last few shillings, but you can never admit it.

" Then you really mean it ?—about being out of a job ? "

" Of course I mean it. Why ? "

" Take me out to dinner, and I'll tell you."

" Love to," I said, " but the way I'm fixed, you'll have to take me."

" You mean you're broke ? " she cried, her eyes wide in astonishment. " Evelyn, why didn't you tell me ? " And she sounded as exasperated and reproachful as she might have done twenty years earlier, on finding me to be involved in some trouble I hadn't confided to her. Dorothy would always give away half of what was hers, if a friend was in need of it. Nobody knew that better than I did. We grew up next door to each other, and were cronies from the days when I was seven and she was six ; and maybe that was why she hadn't been able to think of me as a possible husband. I was too near to her to be seen in a just focus. " Come on, let's go somewhere where we can talk."

We fell into step together, and Dorothy slipped her arm in mine, and drew a deep breath, and the social brightness faded out of her beautiful, clear, tired face.

" Evelyn," she said, " I'm a widow. Did you know? Not grass any more, an ordinary widow."

" Are you proposing to me ? " I asked, interested.

I hadn't meant to say that, it had just slipped out before I was aware. Only once in my life had I ever considered what I was about to say to Dorothy, and look where it got me that time.

" After the last fiasco ? What a hope ! At least, I have got a proposal to make, of a kind, but it's strictly practical. No, it isn't, either," she contradicted herself impulsively the next moment, " it's a matter of needing help, and asking you to help me. Because I always could, and I don't think you've changed, and I don't feel that I've changed much, either, when I'm with you. If you know what I mean."

I knew what she meant.

" Did you know that Bruce was dead ? "

" I read it in some newspaper, about three months ago. He was killed by a fall of stones on some dig in Greece, wasn't he ? I'm sorry, I know you still had a certain feeling for him, even if——"

" Even if we couldn't live together." She gave me a quick glance, and looked away again, and I knew she was remembering as vividly as I was the day when I rushed home on my first leave, in 1941, frightfully self-conscious in my new uniform, and keyed-up for action, heroism and sacrifice. I hardly waited to kiss my mother before hopping over the wall into the doctor's garden, next door, and asking if Dorothy was in. And the same night, in the unfathomable darkness of the blackout that was so unexpectedly friendly to lovers, I asked her to marry me. In what words, thank God, I can't remember; I was never eloquent, and the occasion probably undid me completely. The formula, in any case, couldn't have mattered. The disaster was more fundamental than that.

Dorothy laughed. Looking back on the awful moment from this distance, I could see that it was a laugh of sheer shock and disorientation; she laughed because the earth had reeled under her feet, and she'd lost her bearings. I'd always been there beside her, with her in every predicament her ingenuity and mine could concoct, with her in a sense in which a brother wouldn't have been with her. Brothers and sisters are rivals, and we'd always been allies, without a shadow of rivalry between us. If I'd had the sense to realise and draw back, if I'd given her until my next visit to think about it, everything might have been different. She might have made the essential readjustments, and seen me in a new light, she might even have been delighted with her discovery. But I was affronted, and confused, and I panicked, and pressed her for an answer. Then she said no, definitely, indignantly, shocked at the idea, as if I'd been proposing a kind of incest; and she pulled away from me, and ran into the house. And I was unspeakably hurt and humiliated, and probably so was she. I didn't go near her again, I didn't want to see or hear of her again. But I somehow never looked at anyone else, either.

These things are as delicate and difficult as marriage itself. No wonder I made such a mess of it, at nineteen and a bit, and starting with the disadvantage of being loved already in a different way.

The next leave I had I spent carefully avoiding so much as looking at the house where she lived; and only at the end of it did I find out that I'd been wasting my pains. She'd joined the Nursing Reserve, and gone off to London. Six months later she married Bruce Almond, who was wealthy, and old enough to be her father, and in my distress I liked to think that those were the reasons why she married him. But I always knew better than that. He was experienced, travelled, well known, extremely personable and probably very nice, in his eccentric fashion. He was doing some sort of backroom work on maps and strategy at the time, because he knew the Middle East like the palm of his hand, from pre-war archæological expeditions which were his passion. Passion is the just word. From all accounts he was about as scientific as Schliemann, without even the same fabulous luck; but he was as famous with the lay public as he was notorious among scholars and professional archæologists, at once a legend and a joke.

" Bruce was delightful," said Dorothy in a rush, as though she'd been following my thoughts, " and impossible ! I was terribly in love with him, Evelyn. He was so different from anyone I'd ever known, and his attentions were so flattering, and being with him was such crazy fun. He was a good classical scholar, too—up to a point. It was something incurably juvenile in him that undid all the good effect. What didn't fit in with his ideas he quietly toed under the carpet when he thought you weren't looking. Completely irresponsible. After we were married it was quite easy to bear with him for a while, because we saw each other only now and again, for quite short periods, and even his childish intellectual dishonesty was a joke and a holiday, taken in small doses. And then there was the baby. But after the war, when we were together all the time, it was unbearable. The real baby made it more dreadful than ever, having a middle-aged baby on my hands. I couldn't go on telling fairy-tales and pretending to believe them for ever; and with Crispin I knew it wouldn't be for ever, he was like me, he began to question everything, he'd go on asking why, and raising odd, logical objections until the cows came home. But with Bruce it would have been for ever. To the very end I knew he was nice, and dear, and I liked him. But having to be with him drove me insane. And being with me drove *him* wild, too. I was like a perpetual derisive titter spoiling his best effects, even when I tried to behave like an angel. *He* wasn't a liar or a humbug, he convinced himself every time. But I didn't know how to pretend to be convinced when I wasn't, and every time I tried I felt like a liar and a humbug, so I stopped trying. So you see, it couldn't go on."

"No," I said, rather wanting this to stop, but unwilling to disoblige Dorothy. "I see it couldn't go on. Tell me, are you taking me somewhere, or am I taking you somewhere? There's a little place round this corner, or there used to be, the last time I was here——"

She said that anywhere would do, abstractedly, not turning her mind away from the contemplation of the past. So I took her to the nearest quiet place, which was still where I'd left it, and not even redecorated, and installed her in the quietest corner of it. She detached herself from her regrets, reassessments, whatever they were, long enough to say firmly: "You're dining with me, remember." Then she cupped her chin in her palms, and went back to the story she wanted me, for some reason, to hear and understand.

"When we split up, at the end of 1945, I felt it was all my fault. I had to be free of him, but I didn't want to put the blame on him. I was all for the equality of the sexes, I didn't see why he should shoulder a guilt I felt to be mine. That's why I did the damnfool thing I did do. I knew he needed to be free just as much as I did, and I took it for

granted he'd jump at the chance if I provided it. So I—
I went off with someone else. Never mind who, he was
sweet and kind, and a good friend to me, and anyhow he's
dead now, he got killed climbing some mountain in Austria
two years later. And I wasn't in love with him, and I don't
think he was with me, or I wouldn't have asked him. We
went to a hotel in the Lake District for a week-end, and
provided Bruce with grounds for divorce. I gave him the
proofs, and told him to go ahead, and I wouldn't defend
the case.

" And what do you think ? Bruce didn't believe in
divorce ! Oh, it was genuine, he had religious scruples that
told him he'd taken me for better or for worse. He agreed
it had turned out for worse, for both of us, but even if we
were forced to live apart in order to live at all, we were still
married to each other for good. But he offered me a generous
separation settlement, and told me that I should be joint
heir with Crispin to everything he had. Only, of course,
as I'd admitted misconduct, the settlement would be
conditional on my giving up the boy to him."

" In fact," I said, " you'd put yourself in his power, and
he could dictate his own terms."

" Yes—because if I refused to make a private settlement
as he wished, he could take it to court, and what could they
do but give Crispin to the innocent party ? It would have
come to the same thing in the end, with all the mud and
publicity thrown in. But, Evelyn, it wasn't spite on his
part. You must understand that. There was a good deal
of the Puritan in Bruce, I'd really shocked him, he would
have thought it his duty to keep me from corrupting Crispin
at all costs. And he was generous to me in every other way
—or would have been, if I'd let him. I wouldn't touch his
money. That wasn't spite either, not after the first few
months, at any rate. He paid the allowance into an account
for me regularly. It's still lying there. I didn't hate him for

long, but I couldn't live on a man after I'd stopped living with him."

" So that's how you lost the child," I said. Such rumours as had reached me had said boldly that she'd sold out her interests in her son in return for a money settlement; which had never sounded like Dorothy. But one doesn't expect rumour to be charitable.

" That's how. And the cream of the joke on me, my dear Evelyn, is that nothing whatever happened in that Lakeland hotel—nothing at all! Tony kissed me good night, and slept on the couch. I provided the proofs, all right, only they didn't prove anything, because there was nothing to prove. But they proved it too well for me to be able to withdraw my story afterwards. I couldn't unprove it. I agreed to Bruce's terms. What else could I do? He closed up his house, and went abroad, and took Crispin with him. And I went back to my violin, because I had to have something to live on—and something to live for."

She looked up at me suddenly across her wine-glass with a rather wry smile, her eyes hazy with reminiscence. It was oddly pleasing that she should talk to me so candidly, with so little reserve, the moment we were together again.

" Do you remember how we used to leave a record of Heifetz playing to keep mother happy, while we nipped over the back wall and went up to the woods? Poor mother, how lucky for me she wasn't musical! Nobody else could possibly confuse me with Heifetz. Of course we always got found out as soon as the record stopped, but somehow she always fell for the trick the next time, just the same. What a pity we hadn't got an auto-change on the old radiogram in those days."

" All that practising you never did seems to have stood you in good stead, just the same," I said. " Even in the Sultanate I heard about your triumph."

"I had to have a triumph. Just one, after the biggest failure in the world. I fancy Bruce felt that way too. That's why he plunged into the bowels of Asia Minor with more energy than ever. He didn't find much, but he enjoyed himself a lot, and didn't do much damage. It was his theories that were so unscientific, not his method on a dig. And think of the wonderful life Crispin had, dragged up all over Mesopotamia, and Persia, and Greece, with Bruce a lovely companion, just an older boy, hardly an adult at all. When there was a school within reach, he went to school, but mostly Bruce taught him himself, which means that he learned Greek almost as he learned English. He's done as he pleased, lived just as he pleased, behaved like an infant when he felt like it, and a man when he felt like it. No wonder he adored Bruce. Any boy would."

"He's with you now, I suppose?" I counted up the years she'd been without him. He must be sixteen by this time. "Where are you living?"

"In Bruce's house, in Somerset; Chilcot Mendip's the name of the village. He left the house to me," she said in a low voice, staring into her glass. "He didn't have time to make other dispositions for Crispin, or I expect he would have. You know how he died? A stone lintel fell on him, one night when he was roaming about the site alone. They found him crushed to death under half a ton of stone. I rushed there as soon as I could, and brought Crispin home. The Greek authorities were very kind, and made everything easy for us."

"Everything except getting to know your own son!" I thought, but didn't say. I had a feeling she was going to say it for me the next minute, and she did.

"Evelyn, I'm having son trouble. Are you any good with sons?"

"I don't know. I've never had any."

She blinked at that, and devoted herself for a minute to

the peeling of a pear. "Fair enough," she said at last.
"I asked for that."

"Tell me about him. You're going to, anyhow. Go on,
I'll buy it."

She didn't need any more encouragement, she poured it
all out gratefully. Considering the life the boy had led, there
was nothing surprising in what she had to say about him.

"He was very much attached to his father, you see, and
they've lived on the most intimate terms for twelve years,
without having to share each other with anyone else. In all
those years he hasn't seen me even once, I'm a stranger, and
nothing more. I've tried not to make any great claims on
him, not too soon. But still he isn't settling down as he
should. I sent him to Bruce's old school, I thought the
mere fact that Bruce went there would reconcile him.
I ought to have known it wouldn't be so simple. After being
treated like a contemporary, and responsible, how could he
possibly accept the juvenile sort of values and disciplines
that are quite proper to schools ? You can't just voluntarily
become unsophisticated once you *are* sophisticated, can
you ? It all seemed so absurd and pretentious to him, such
a waste of time. He—well, he——"

"He absconded," I said.

"Within a week. After they'd stretched every possible
point to take him at short notice, because of Bruce ! I'd
have sent him back, but he said he'd only do the same again,
as often as I made it necessary. And I knew he would. So
what was the use ? I sent him to the local grammar school.
Academically he's years ahead of his age in most subjects,
and years behind in a few—the scientific ones that didn't
interest Bruce. But he wouldn't have the local school either.
He couldn't exactly abscond from there. He just set to work
to subvert the whole place. They stood him for three weeks,
and then it was clear that his endurance was longer than
theirs. So they informed me that they could do nothing

with him, since he was quite determined not to co-operate. And would I please take him away. And I did. What else could I do? "

The only alternative course which immediately suggested itself to me was not one that would have commended itself to Dorothy, so I refrained from mentioning it. On second thoughts I didn't think much of it myself. There was something to be said for the boy, after all. Dorothy was right, when you've been made into something quite unsuitable for school life you can't unmake yourself and do the job over again.

" You want him to go on to a university, of course ? "

" It would be a cruel waste if he didn't. He's brilliant, Evelyn. It isn't partiality, he really is brilliant."

" Then the only thing I can see for it," I said, " is private coaching. Get him a resident tutor, and let them fight it out."

" I did," said Dorothy, almost complacently. " Crispin won. It took him a month to drive the man out of the house, but he did it."

" The tutor must have been a poor fish," I said unguardedly, " to let a sixteen-year-old get the better of him."

" He was quite a good man. You're underestimating Crispin, I'm afraid."

" He wouldn't drive me out of the house," I maintained, even more unwisely, and saw a smile quiver irresistibly at the corner of her lips for a moment before she smoothed it away.

" I don't suppose he would," she agreed too docilely. " That's why I was so awfully glad to discover that you were free. Evelyn, I've got a wonderful idea."

Then I knew what she was about; and as in the old days, I was practically disarmed before she even asked what she wanted of me.

" As I remember it," I said resignedly, and more prophetically than I realised, "your wonderful ideas always used to end up in my getting tanned—'for leading Dorothy into mischief'!"

She laughed, knowing already that she had only to ask, that there was nothing I could refuse her. She stretched out her hand across the table, and laid it over mine, and as suddenly as it had come the laughter was gone. This was a desperately serious business for her, there was no mistaking that.

"Evelyn, I've never got over the feeling that I let Bruce down. It's worse now he's dead, you see, because now it's too late to make amends. But it makes me feel more strongly than ever that I've got to do better for Crispin. At least I shall be doing something for his father if I can put things right for him. I came to London just to attend Professor Barclay's lecture, all on Bruce's account. It sounds silly, but I did. He's *the* authority on Bruce's subject, you see, and Bruce admired him so childishly, and was so hungry for his good opinion—I don't know, I suppose I was hoping he'd let fall a small tribute to Bruce in his lecture somewhere, but of course he didn't. Probably quite justly—but even experts must have some human frailties, and I thought that just now—Bruce being so recently dead—— He did write me quite a nice letter after the tragedy, saying he'd heard I was left with a son to launch in the world, and if there was anything he could do to help, to further his prospects in any way—— I had to explain that Crispin was still at school. It was only a conventional letter, but I was touched. I wanted Crispin to come to town with me for the lecture, I thought of introducing myself and him, just in case he might respond a little more warmly to someone Bruce had admired and talked about. If they'd hit it off I meant to hang on to the acquaintance, and maybe ask the Professor down to Somerset sometimes. But Crispin refused to come. And after I'd even gone to the trouble to read through his new book ! " she said with a rueful smile, and turned it so that I could see the austere title, offset in white on black, *The Fall of the House of Atreus,* and the photograph of the author, lean and authoritative and himself Olympian, with his crisp grey hair and his clipped moustache, and his hard, light stare under the thick brows.

" Not the most approachable of men," I suggested gently, thinking now with astonishment and pain of Dorothy hesitating in the shadows like a shy schoolgirl.

" No, I saw it wouldn't really have been any good. They're not human, not really. But after all it didn't matter. I was luckier even than I'd hoped. I met you instead."

Her hand lay still upon mine. " Evelyn, will you come and act as Crispin's tutor ? At a fair salary, of course, I won't have you except on a business footing, it wouldn't be honest. You're a classics man, you're perfectly competent to coach him, but that's the very least of it. He needs a man to be his friend. He's always been with men. You could win his confidence, and help him to come to terms with a world without Bruce, and—and with me. Evelyn, Crispin doesn't like me ! On Bruce's account, I suppose. And I do need an ally so badly, and I'd so much rather have you than any old Professor Barclay. Come to Somerset with me to-morrow. Once he's adjusted himself, you needn't stay his tutor a day longer than you want to—but I hope you'll always be his friend."

Come to Somerset, I thought. Well, why not ? Nobody in this country was waiting for me. No job was being kept open for me. As well Somerset and Dorothy as any other solution. If I could really be of help to Dorothy, that was all the inducement I needed.

About the boy, as yet, I hadn't thought seriously at all.

" I'll come," I said, and we shook hands on it.

CHAPTER II

BRUCE ALMOND had left plenty of money behind him, to judge by the Jaguar Dorothy drove. Or perhaps that was one of the products of her personal career. We made good time on the journey, and were turning into the drive of the Lawns, at Chilcot Mendip, by half past three. It was a big house, plain and foursquare in the middle of a shaven plane of grass, but with belts of shrubbery and trees round the margin of its garden on all sides. It stood on the edge of the limestone hills, with the village, which was almost large enough to be considered a market town, just below it in a hollow of the slopes, sheltered by a shallow escarpment.

There was one gardener cruising along the vast lawns with a motor-mower, and another at work among the flower-beds that fringed the drive. The Georgian frontage of the house rose three stories, tier beyond tier of nicely modulated windows mounting to the ruled roof and the wide parapet.

" Bruce's money keeps it up," said Dorothy, reading my thoughts. " I felt that was fair enough. What I make keeps me, but it wouldn't keep the Lawns. And this place will be Crispin's, some day. As far as I'm concerned, it's in trust, that's all." Astonishingly humble and characteristically arrogant at the same time, she set out her position clearly, so that no one who had the slightest concern in her affairs could possibly be under any misapprehension.

" Bruce's archæological exploits began up there," she said, waving a hand towards the hill that continued its terraced rise beyond the house. " There are caves, if you're interested. He used to go and dredge up a few poor little relics there when he was a boy. But the nearest one's

23

tricky, so I'm told, and never was inhabited by our ancestors. Of course, our caverns are small beer by comparison with Cheddar and Wookey Hole. No visitors ever come near them."

There was nothing in the slightest degree sinister or oppressive about the house. It stood solidly rooted in its acres of grass, with all the enormous self-confidence of the eighteenth century. But that rising slope of broken hillside beyond, striated with the naked levels of limestone in its upper reaches, and grey through its thin grass right to the sheltering belt of trees, gave the place an air of being besieged unawares by some ancient enemy. The longer I looked at it, the more incongruous seemed the self-satisfied face of the house, staring so blandly in the opposite direction, towards the security of the little town.

"Don't you find yourself inconveniently far from London here?" I asked. "In your profession I should have thought that might be a handicap."

"I haven't accepted any bookings since I came home, as a matter of fact," owned Dorothy rather wryly. "I wanted to get Crispin settled, and let him get used to me. I don't know that I want to spend all my life here, but I can afford a few years." She encountered my eyes, not too happily, and smiled. "I know! Fame won't wait around for me for ever. But I can't help it. Crispin's an inescapable fact. We came here because it was his father's home, and the place where he wanted to be."

"Let's go and find him," I said. "I'm getting curious about this boy of yours."

She chattered so feverishly, as we went into the house, that I knew she was nervous about the meeting, and it seemed to me an impertinence in a brat of sixteen to upset that immaculate poise which must have been the despair of so many distinguished adult males. But for the moment she was wasting her qualms. There was no boy in the hall to meet her, no boy in the large, sunny drawing-room, no boy in the cosier garden-room, no boy in the library. Certain signs of him appeared in this last room, it's true. The leather-topped table in the tall window-embrasure held a small pile of books, and one volume turned down upon the dark red hide, as though he had abandoned his reading only a little while ago ; not to mention a cigarette-box and an ash-tray containing half a dozen cigarette-ends.

" His ? " I asked.

" Sure to be. Bruce let him smoke, it's too late for anyone else to revoke the permit now. He doesn't smoke many. But he would if I tried to forbid it."

It was certainly pointless to be indignant about so natural a reaction. " And this is his choice of reading ? " There was a notebook lying beside the pile, but I didn't touch it. His belongings were left in position with an altogether adult assumption that they would be respected. But I did look at the spine of the book he'd been reading. I don't know what I'd expected, but it certainly hadn't been Sophocles. " Whatever his objections to school," I said, " and tutors, they don't appear to include an antipathy to study."

" He reads a lot. And invariably above my head. I think this is the one place where he's almost happy. Roving round the Middle East can be quite a comfortable sort of life, but it does preclude carrying a large library with vou. Will you excuse me, Evelyn, I'd better go and see where he's got to. I expect Mrs. Hallam will know."

She came back ten minutes later, looking at once humiliated and resigned. " Mrs. Hallam says he went out after lunch. He didn't say where, and he didn't say when he'd be back. She asked him, and he declined to discuss his business with her."

" In short," I said, " this is the first blow struck in his campaign against me."

" I'm afraid not, because when I telephoned this morning

I didn't tell him a word about you. No, it's merely the latest
blow in his campaign against me."

There was nothing to be done about it but wait for him
to come in. In the meantime, I installed myself next door
to the boy's bedroom, a location which I personally felt
might be a mistake, but that was how Dorothy had arranged
things. She showed me Crispin's room. Apart from a great
many books, stacked tightly and tidily away on their shelves,
it had nothing remarkable about it, and very little that was
personal and could give it individuality. It looked as if he
had made no attempt to make a permanent place for himself
and his belongings, but was simply using the room to sleep
in until events moved him on to some other, undisclosed
milieu. Like a student's hostel room—no, far less personal
than that, for there were no trophies of his past life, no
group photographs to give him a background.

The only entirely individual thing visible, apart from the
books, was one photograph which stood on a table by the
window, turned to catch a good light. I recognised Bruce
Almond's handsome, thin, enthusiast's face, with the rich
tan, the semi-military moustache, the ardent blue eyes ;
behind him the arid, eroded soil of Greece, a fragmentary
white wall, and that blinding air, sharp as diamonds. Was it
that air that made looking for the ultimate truth so natural
a part of the Greek mind ? That crystal brilliance invited
the eye to penetrate the remotest of distances, why should
not the spirit follow ? Not that Bruce's far-sighted blue eyes
had been looking for any ultimate truth, according to
Dorothy. But as for the boy, he was her son, too.

He didn't come in until late in the evening. Dorothy and
I had dined together, and but for the anxiety which haunted
her, I personally could have enjoyed the tête-à-tête ; but
her mind was away with the errant son. Afterwards we sat
in the garden-room, and Dorothy played. She was too dis-
tracted to do herself justice, but even so I could see some-

thing of the quality which had brought her into the front rank so quickly. She had a fastidious delicacy of taste that robbed that most perilous of instruments of all its offensiveness, for every temptation to emotionalism, over-statement and self-assertion she rejected by instinct. The violin is a graceful instrument, too, and Dorothy's own purity of line as she played duplicated the clarity of her melodic line. It seemed to me that it must be a very odd sixteen-year-old who could resist feeling proud of such a mother.

We were sitting almost in the dark, playing records on the radiogram, when I heard the faintest of movements in the open window that gave on to the garden and, turning my head, saw the figure of the boy against the lambent July sky. He had approached very quietly, and Dorothy had not heard him come. She sat with her elbows on the arm of her chair, and her chin in her hands, her eyes fixed on the minute glow of the 'gram's glass face; and the boy stood in the open window, as intently watching her. I was less directly in his line of vision, and screened from the glow of light, and because of our concentration on the music there had been no exchange of voices to give him warning. But in any case he was so unwaveringly engrossed in her that I doubt if he would have noticed me.

A slender figure, less than the average height for his years; a very trim and taut manner of carrying himself, and a poise of the head that reminded me of Dorothy even in silhouette. That was all I could see, until some sense of his presence penetrated her absorption, and she looked up and exclaimed : " Crispin ! " and jumped up to switch on the lights. Then, because I was already watching him, I had time to catch the last glimmer of the unguarded face, just stripped of the covering darkness, before he drew down over it, with unchildlike readiness and resolution, the cool composure behind which it seemed he habitually hid. The change was so rapid that the effect was like a lightning-flash, revealing him but blinding me for one instant. The eyes, dark and abnormally dilated as they sprang out of the dark, stared fierily for a fraction of a second, and then were merely rather pleasing eyes, not unlike Dorothy's but blue rather than violet, blinking composedly at the sudden radiance of the lamp. The fierce, drawn lines of the still face, all bone like Bruce's face, mellowed into an austere but serene calm.

" Good evening ! " said Crispin. " I hope you had a nice trip ? "

He looked older than his years, perhaps a willowy eighteen. It wasn't the effect of his clothes, though the nicely-tailored grey slacks and heather tweed sportscoat, the open-necked shirt and silk scarf, were the approved wear for anyone from seventeen to seventy. It was rather something about Crispin himself that gave him those borrowed years. In spite of his smallness he looked more formed, in body and face, than a sixteen-year-old should look, moved with a compact and decided authority very unlike the coltish clumsiness of most boys, and concealed himself behind the civilised neutrality of a man's self-possession.

" Crispin, where have you been ? " cried Dorothy, already angry now that she no longer had to be anxious. " I expected to see you when I got back this afternoon. I told you I should be home before tea."

" You didn't say you wanted me to be here," he said, raising his eyebrows a little.

" Naturally I wanted you to be here. Did it need to be said ? Come in and close the window." And when he had obeyed her, which he did at once, she turned to me, and he, following the movement, noticed me for the first time. " Mr. Manville, this is my son Crispin."

The look he gave me measured me, weighed me, declared war on me, set me miles and miles away from him ; an astonishing look, brilliant, fierce and resentful, while face

and voice remained all distant civility. " I beg your pardon ! "
he said. " My mother didn't tell me she was bringing a
guest down with her." And, without advancing a step, he
gave me a small, grave and polite bow, effectively fending
off any possibility of being approached or touched.

" Mr. Manville is your new tutor," said Dorothy dryly.

The news appeared to afford him a certain relief, presumably because it enabled him to place me. At any rate,
I could only call the change that came into his eyes relief,
combined with a slightly contemptuous hostility. He had
such command over his face that only the eyes were any
index to his mind. Remarkably fine eyes in a clear but
undistinguished face, eyes that seemed a lighter, shallower
blue now that he had the situation well in hand.

" I hope my mother made it clear that the job isn't a
sinecure ? " he said, in the lightly social tone of one making
conversation at a party. " You accepted it with your eyes
open ? "

" Oh, yes," I assured him, " I know the odds."

" Then I think it's sporting of you to take it on." He
went across to the cabinet on the other side of the room,
and helped himself to vermouth, which I think was as far
as he dared go. He wanted to be as provoking as possible,
without actually overstepping the mark at which his mother
would feel compelled to pick up his gage. But he wasn't
as unmoved as he pretended. I'd been a shock to him ; and
for one who had been informed of the difficulties I wasn't
talking enough to reassure him, wasn't being sufficiently
firm, soothing and schoolmasterly. " She told you the last
one cracked up in a month ? " he asked, with his back
turned on us.

" Oh, he probably had scruples against taking your
mother's money on false pretences. My terms of reference
are rather different. It's all one to me whether you want to
learn anything or not. Time's no object."

It was to him, though. I saw his shoulders stiffen. But all he said was : " Can I get you a drink? I suppose we may as well consider to-night a truce."

Dorothy said gently : " Crispin, dear, don't go on with this stupidity. No one's trying to force you into a school now. There's no reason whatever why you should refuse the opportunity to go on with your education here at home. You know quite well your father would have wanted you to follow him to Oxford and take your degree. Don't you want to do as he would have wished ? "

He turned and looked at her with the glass in his hand, and said no word. There was no guessing what was going on in his mind ; but it was revealing that he didn't at once say : No !

" You have the ability, and I can't believe you'd be so stupid or so wicked as to throw it away. So you need some-one to help you. Why not be sensible, and get to know Mr. Manville before you set out on a course you'll regret ? How do you know what you may not be wasting if you refuse this chance ? "

" I need no help from anyone," he said, slowly and firmly.

" You're not such a fool as to believe that," said Dorothy, rising from her chair with a creditable smile and only a suppressed sigh. " Well, I'm going to bed. I'll leave you to come to terms as best you can. Good night, Mr. Man-ville ! Good night, darling ! "

He turned his cheek mildly for her kiss, submitting with a resigned face, such as most boys proffer for the salutation of female relatives. But even from where I sat I could feel the tension that stiffened his body.

When she was gone he came and dropped into a chair opposite mine, and said, with so punctilious a candour that he might as well have spared all his later efforts to make himself offensive : " I'm sorry, I hope you understand there's nothing personal in this. But I don't want a tutor, and I won't have one. I've no intention of studying, and I don't want you here."

" What's your objection to studying ? " I asked.

" Just that for me there's no point in it."

" That comes well," I said, " from someone who reads Sophocles in the original Greek for pleasure."

" Yes, for pleasure. It just happens that I do get pleasure out of that."

" Good! Then what's wrong with reading Greek together until it just happens that something else gives you pleasure ? "

" I won't co-operate," he said, voice and colour rising, and shut his lips firmly.

" All right, if that's how you want it. But effective or not, I shall still be here—which I think is what you chiefly resent. Wouldn't it pay you to make the best of it, instead of the worst ? "

He made no answer.

" Very well, I'll consider war declared. At what hour in the morning would you like the first battle to take place ? "

" It makes no difference," he said in a very clipped voice. " I shan't be here."

" If you mean by that," I said, though I was feeling my way more gingerly than I would have liked him to know, " that you intend to abscond from the Lawns, frankly, I don't believe you. I think that's the last thing you'll consider, for reasons best known to yourself. But if you mean you won't turn up at—let's say half past nine, shall we ?— here, in this room, ready for action, I can only say that you might as well. You'll be here soon afterwards, if I have to carry you."

He flushed, but he didn't exclaim uselessly, and to judge by his angry but shrewd stare, he was in no doubt of the result if it came to a clash. He knew only too well the inadequacy of his body as yet to match the scope of his mind, and he had sense enough not to ignore facts, even when he was angry.

" When you get me here," he said, gnawing his lip, " you'll be no nearer getting me to work."

" That's up to you. But you'll be extremely bored by lunch-time. And still more bored in the afternoon."

" So will you," he said, reasonably enough.

" I can console myself with the thought that I'm being paid for it. But you wòn't have any such consolation."

" And how long do you propose to keep that up ? "

" As long as you make it necessary."

He gave me a long, level stare from eyes now almost black with anger and anxiety, thrust himself to his feet, and marched out without another word.

CHAPTER III

GET HIM A TUTOR, I'd said, and let 'em fight it out. Crispin and I fought it out for nearly three weeks with varying tactics and no decisive battles, both saving our strength for the classical opportunity that didn't come. He was a master of exasperation, I could well imagine the frame of mind in which my predecessor had resigned his appointment, and gratefully shaken off the dust of Chilcot Mendip while he was still sane. But that course wasn't open to me. I'd taken on quite a different job, one I couldn't resign. Still, I couldn't say I hadn't asked for it.

The strangest thing was that I liked the little devil, and admired his tenacity, even when I was longing to wring his neck.

For a week he concentrated on being missing whenever he was expected to be with me. Each time I ran him patiently to earth, with all the more assurance once I'd had a couple of trial runs, and verified my hunch that he never went very far from the house, and brought him back and impounded him in the library, tacking on to his imprisonment the time he'd been missing. Whatever means of transport were available to him at the house I contrived to get under lock and key, and in a few days I grew expert in forecasting where he would be. I didn't cheat by spying on him beforehand, and once the fixed school hours were over I didn't play watchdog any longer. I just saw to it that he sat through the appointed time with nothing whatever to occupy him but the studies he refused to touch. His resolution didn't waver, either. He didn't tempt providence by resisting, once he was run to earth, but rose and came with me, with lifted eyebrows and curling lip. But once inside the library he would sit without uttering a word, without opening a book himself or accepting one from me, and without acknowledging my presence at his elbow by more than an occasional brushing glance. It wasn't as easy as he pretended, and he wasn't happy with the method, it was too inactive for his nature, and was having a more disastrous effect on him than it was on me. I went on offering him books, because the temptation to accept them and join in was visibly growing stronger; and I went on delivering, as eloquently as I could with such a stony audience, the lectures on history and literature and art to which he refused to pay attention. To try to draw observations from him was useless, but he couldn't help hearing my expositions; and there were times when, for all his fixed, impervious face, I knew his interest was caught, and he was an intent, if unwilling, listener.

I was winning this round, slowly and uphill every inch of the way, but I was winning, and he knew it. He changed his tactics. From silent he became voluble, and from well-mannered, not without a fearful effort, the most boorish sixteen-year-old imaginable. Every word he spoke to me

was calculated insolence. He might have been studying the
art of needling his teachers and elders all his young life, he
was so good at it. Still worse, he extended his general bad
behaviour to include Dorothy, and very quickly grasped that
he could make himself still more offensive to me by making
himself offensive to her. Very often his natural good
manners nearly lifted him out of his chair when she entered
the room, and it was hard work not to put out his cigarette
when she came in, and not to jump to light hers on the rare
occasions when she smoked ; but he managed to restrain
himself, and stick to the rôle he'd chosen. There were times
when he came pretty near to getting a thundering good
hiding ; probably the only reason he didn't was that his own
crudities jarred on him as much as anybody, and he could
never quite disguise the fact. The appalled distaste in his
eyes, the flush he couldn't quite suppress, always side-
tracked me from exasperation into curiosity. Why go to
such pains simply to maintain an objection to my presence ?
Was it as vital as all that to get me out of the house ? By
that time this puzzle alone would have been enough to keep
me from going.

It was in the last week of July that this phase came to a
head. Dorothy was opening her letters at breakfast, and
Crispin, who was making a point of being annoyingly late
for meals, among other things, came in just in time to hear
her say, as she unfolded the last letter : " I thought I knew
the handwriting ! Dermot's back in England ! "

The name meant nothing to me, but it meant something
to the boy. I heard his steps halt at my back, where he was
just crossing to his chair ; I felt him stiffen into stillness.
I couldn't turn to look at his face, but I knew how it would
look, tight and motionless, with tensed mouth, and eyes
half-hooded under his long lashes, very dark with awareness. He had command of himself in a moment, and moved
on and sat down in his place, and by the time he was there

in front of my eyes he was looking nothing but sleepy, and withdrawn, and rather cross, as though he had awakened very late, and risen without waiting to complete the process.

The tension was still in him, though. I was glad that Dorothy seemed less sensitive to it than I was, perhaps because she found it difficult to think of him as anything but a child.

" Dermot ? " I said. " Should I know him? "

" No, I'm sorry, I was thinking aloud. Dermot Crane. He was my husband's right-hand man at Pirithoön. He stayed on in Greece when we left, and he's just come home. He wants to come for a week-end. Crispin knows him well, of course. It'll be nice to see Dermot again, won't it, darling ? ". And she looked across at him with an eagerness which was pathetic in such an imperious creature, hoping for a spark of pleasure, at least.

He looked back at her with eyes like dark pebbles, and said without the least expression : " Will it ? "

" Oh, of course," she said, recoiling into the uneasily light, bright tolerance she had taken to practising towards him when he was difficult, " if you've got out of bed on the wrong side, we'll say no more about it. Nothing's nice when you're in that mood."

" You're going to write and tell him to come, of course, in any case," said Crispin coldly. " It isn't my welcome he'll be worrying about."

She gave him a doubtful, frowning look at that, but it could have meant much or nothing at all, and she thought she was becoming hypersensitive from sheer fondness. But when she rose from the table and passed behind him to go into the garden, she stopped at his back, and let her hands rest on his shoulders, looking down at him with such unguarded affection and anxiety that very little was left intact of the superb, public Dorothy.

" Darling, I do wish——"

I don't know what she was going to say; perhaps she herself didn't know what came after that, for she stopped there, and heaved a great, helpless sigh, and then, having run out of coherent words, surrendered to the longing to let her touch express what her tongue found inexpressible. She bent her head, kissed his averted temple, where the dark, wavy hair sprang fine as down, and then shut her arm round his shoulders, and drew his cheek against hers.

For a moment I thought he was going to accept the embrace. He wavered, he almost leaned to her touch; and then the expected happened. He recollected himself with a convulsion like the recoil from a precipice, and went rigid in her arm, his cheek hard against hers, muscles tensed, brows drawn tightly together as though in a spasm of rage or pain. He put up his hands, and pushed her away from him violently.

" Don't ! " It was a cry of panic, soft though it was ; but what followed was calculated, and cold, and quietly vicious. He stared up at her with a pinched white face, and said venomously : " Don't practise on *me* ! I draw the line at serving as one of your guinea-pigs, even if Dermot is coming for the week-end. If you want to be in form for him, there's always Mr. Manville, I don't suppose he'd mind pacing you."

Dorothy took her hands from him as though he had scorched her fingers, and stood white and trembling, staring down into a white, trembling face suddenly the image of her own. He had frightened himself horribly. The minute it was out he looked as if he would have liked to vanish, to die, to be invisible, to be turned to stone, anything to lose the knowledge of what he'd said, and the awareness of our having heard it. But there it was, still burning on the air, and there was no pretending it hadn't happened, and no letting it pass. Some things will go away if they're ignored long enough. This one wouldn't. And the tears in Dorothy's eyes floated me into action almost before I knew how angry I was.

I came out of my chair in one lunge, and hoisted him out of his by the scruff of the neck. " Excuse us ! " I remember saying to Dorothy in the most matter-of-fact of voices. " We have pressing business." We had, too. This time he was going to answer questions if I had to shake every word out of him. This time I was going to get the truth. This time he was going to tell me why he wanted the ground round him cleared of all strangers, and what he had against his mother, and who on earth put whatever it was into his fool head. He was going to tell me, or else !

That was positively all I had in mind when I ran him up the stairs ; what he thought was about to happen to him I can only guess. After all, there was a scared kid somewhere inside this rather obnoxious young man. At any rate, on the landing, almost in the doorway of his bedroom, he suddenly turned into a fluid burden, dead weight in my hand, and collapsed at my feet, where as abruptly he became whalebone, dragged down on my wrist with all his might, and tried to spill me over his head. It wasn't a bad attempt, either, and if my reactions hadn't been, as they usually are, reasonably quick, he'd have brought it off. As it was, he only hacked my ankle rather painfully with the heel of his shoe, and jarred my elbow against the frame of the door. But I'm human, and it was enough.

I hoisted him from the floor like a sack, pitched him face downwards on his bed, and gave him a mild sample of what I'd been saving up for him for three weeks. I hadn't lost my temper, and nothing was much hurt but his dignity, but that took a fearful pasting. He went quite rigid with outrage, and then, instead of trying to free himself from the hand I had firmly in his collar, clamped his own hand round my wrist again, and hurled himself bodily off the far side of the bed, trying to drag me with him. He hadn't the weight for it; and instead of holding him back I loosed my hold, and helped him on his way with a hearty hoist. His grip gave, and he fell with a flat thud that knocked the breath out of him. I had plenty of time to step round the bed and sling him back on to it, and there I held him down one-handed, waiting to see how many more little tricks of the kind he had in his repertoire.

He had quite a number, and was game to try them all. He was no longer merely defending himself, but doing his damnedest to defeat me, and what animated him wasn't fright, but sheer flaming temper. He wore himself out trying to break my grip, and I was content simply to counter every trick he threw at me, and hold him floundering in the shambles we'd made of the bed. It went on for some time ; and at what precise stage it ceased to be war to the knife, and became a rough-and-tumble almost for fun, I never quite knew. All I knew was that suddenly I could hear him gasping and gurgling in the pillow, and quaking under my hand as I held him, and for a moment I was afraid I'd driven him to tears of humiliation. In which case I doubt if he would ever have forgiven me. But then I realised that he was laughing. The two are pretty close, in the circumstances ; and the thing to do now was to end the bout quickly, while he was still laughing.

"Had enough ? " I invited him, almost like a contemporary.

"Yes," he gasped from the pillow. He could afford to be a realist if the thing had found its way to a playful level, though I think he was as puzzled as I was as to how and when and why it had resolved itself into a game. "All right—I give you best ! Let me up ! "

"You won't run away ? Give me your parole for ten minutes, and I'm satisfied."

"All right, I promise ! "

I took my hands from him, and went and sat down on the

opposite side of the room. He emerged panting from the rumpled pillows, shook himself into some semblance of tidiness, and combed his tousled hair. The laughter lingered in a faintly awed, faintly rueful grin. He slanted a half-embarrassed glance across the room at me, and blurted out : " I say, you're *good* ! " It was the first time I'd ever heard him sound sixteen, and it was a revelation.

" You're not bad yourself," I said, being carefully off-hand about it. " Who taught you ? "

" Stavros. He was Bruce's foreman at Pirithoön, where the dig was." He was actually talking, voluntarily, without any intent to deceive or annoy. " He used to teach his son Nikos all kinds of fine things, and while he was with us he took me on, too. He treated me just like an extra son. Stavros was fine ! But I believe you could have stood up to him."

In some obscure but quite effective way, everything I'd meant to say to him had become irrelevant ; the ticking-off certainly, the questions hardly less so. I said what seemed to me to be needed most, looking straight into his eyes, clean through the slightly offended but good-humoured laughter on the surface to the shadowy, self-contained depths behind. " I could be quite useful," I said, " in an emergency. If you should be looking for reinforcements, Crispin."

Almost reluctantly he withdrew again into his own lone-liness, and folded himself about whatever he guarded there ; but it seemed to me that he hesitated about closing the door.

" Yes," he said, after a long silence, " I think you could be. If you were on my side." And slowly, ruefully, the door did close against me. I caught, as it were, a glimpse of his face, old with anxiety and worn with longing, as he shut me out. He was dying for a confidant, if only there could be one soul in the world he could trust, but there wasn't. " But you wouldn't be," he said with finality.

" You're mistaken. I'm on your side already. When you want me, I shall be here."

He finished settling his hair, and didn't reply. In a way his desolation seemed aggravated now by the loss even of his hostility to me. That was one war that was over. Not won, but over. It would be absurd and inappropriate to continue his campaign of attrition after this scene. He couldn't get rid of me, and he couldn't let me in. Not yet.

" Aren't you going to bawl me out for being such an oaf to my mother ? " he asked, in a precariously light voice.

" No. There's no need now."

" I was," said Crispin, too loudly and defiantly because of the effort it cost him to say it at all.

" I know. I heard you. You were. But on the other hand, you're not. You can't be surprised if observant people wonder about the discrepancy."

He didn't answer that. He sat on the edge of the bed, with his face turned rather carefully away from me and away from the light, until the ten minutes was up. " May I go now ? "

" Go ahead ! I'll follow you."

I wouldn't have watched him, but it so happened that Dorothy was crossing the hall, and he didn't have to go and look for her, so that I was on the landing when they met. She would have passed him without a word or a glance, frozen into her own anguish, afraid to draw too near him, but he advanced wincingly into her path.

" Mother——! " It only struck me then that it was the first time I'd ever heard him call her that, and even now the word came from his lips stiffly, as though surrounded by quotation marks. " Mother—I shouldn't have spoken to you like that. I'm very sorry."

He leaned forward, and kissed her on the cheek. He had to raise himself slightly on his toes to do it, for she was taller than he was. Then he slipped past her, and almost ran into the library. When I went down, Dorothy was standing where he'd left her, clutching the roses she'd brought in from the garden, and looking dazed, and hopeful, and about to be glad, as if she'd seen an angel.

Crispin was in the library, already sitting at the table, staring beneath a level dark line of brows at his own linked hands. He was walled-in again, the portcullis was down, the drawbridge up, the moat brimming, watchmen on the ramparts. But this time, when I slid a book towards him and invited him to open it, though he scowled at it blackly, his hand went out slowly and opened it.

Maybe I'm not as simple as Dorothy ; certainly I wasn't as happy. " I shouldn't have spoken .to you like that. I'm very sorry." He had apologised for offending against his own idea of himself, yes. But he hadn't withdrawn a word of what he'd said.

CHAPTER IV

Now THAT WE'D achieved at any rate mutual tolerance, I set out to make a conquest of Crispin. If he liked judo, at least that was something I was good for. And Bruce's caves ought to hold attractions for Bruce's son. As long as we stuck to these innocuous pursuits, I felt, as long as I asked no questions until I could feel that he was waiting for them and wanting them, we could at least strike up some kind of a friendship.

And it was easy, easier than I'd hoped. No admittance beyond a certain gate, of course, but up to that point he met me readily. We wrestled, and I put him down gently enough to square with my own conscience, and hard enough to satisfy his ego, and once at least I let him put me down, though the suspicion and offence he manifested made me resolve not to do it again, and once, by a beautiful fluke, he put me down even when I wasn't intending that he should, which atoned for the other mistake, and reduced him to his proper years for five glorious minutes. And we explored the caves, beginning with the one in which Bruce had picked up his first modest relics, and ending with the one Dorothy had described as tricky. That was the one Crispin wanted, naturally, once the idea was put into his head, and he was boy enough to want it at once.

It was quite a cave in its way, but without any spectacular limestone formations to make it popular. The entrance was in a broken outcrop of rock in a thin copse, on the crest of the hill above the house. There was a low rock archway, and then an almost vertical shaft for twenty feet or so. We took plenty of torches and lamps and ropes and various equipment with us, and roped the route methodically as we went, so that getting out was merely a matter of climbing a short fixed ladder. Below the shaft there was a rather nondescript little chamber, uneven and ugly and full of water-drips, and at the end of it a first moderate-sized gallery opened out, with a broken gulf in one side of it. There was only one way on from there, and that was down, through an inverted funnel like the neck of an oubliette. It was wet and slippery, and very dirty, and the air below was intensely cold. We tried our longest rope ladder, and it wasn't long enough, but by joining up two we got down it, maybe fifty feet or more, into an enormous hall fringed along one side with muddy-coloured limestone formations, and on the other with a roaring darkness. The drop appeared to be sheer all along this gulf, our strongest torches couldn't penetrate to the bottom, and there was certainly a lot of water down there, some underground stream bellowing in the dark. There was no way out there. We did find a child-size tunnel in the far end of the hall, and tried out the first few yards of it, and there was certainly fresh air getting into it from somewhere ; but it grew far too tight for me, and I refused to let Crispin try it alone. We fixed our ladders in position on the second visit, and left them there, and made a cache of torches and ropes and soiled overalls in the upper gallery.

The boy was good company on an expedition like that, sensible enough to obey orders without question, and bold enough to think and act for himself where necessary ; and as far as I could see, either entirely without fear, or else he trusted me, at least in these practical affairs, to an extremely flattering degree upon such short acquaintance. I suppose you can get to know someone rather well, and find out exactly how reliable he is, while you're conducting a war against him.

He talked freely, too, now that he'd resigned himself to my being there ; except, of course, that he didn't talk about his mother, or his father, or Dermot Crane, or the dig at Pirithoön, or the secret life that went on inside him. Only once did he say anything which could even be regarded as stemming from that closed and sealed place, and that was when I asked him, unwisely as I thought then and still think, whether he still wanted me to go away. He looked past me through the open window, unsmiling, and said sombrely : " It's too late now. You'll have to take your chance." Perhaps he expected me to ask him more ; perhaps he even wanted it, in a way ; but for the first time I felt that I'd been prying unjustifiably, and in a manner unworthily indirect, and I let it go at that.

That was on the Thursday evening, as he went up to bed. The good night scene was almost invariable, and grew nightly more painful to watch, perhaps because those few weeks of living in close proximity to Dorothy had revived in me an intense appreciation of the value of her affection, and to see her peck sadly, almost timidly, at that little wretch's coldly proffered cheek, hoping hungrily for a little quickening warmth and never getting it, made my heart shrink with sympathetic despair. I tried to suppress it, because I felt the implied humiliation to Dorothy keenly; but circumstances all too often conspired to make me a witness of the ritual, and the stab never failed to get home. He approached her to be kissed, I was persuaded, only in order to avoid some other inevitable emotional contact which might be even more difficult to bear. And he suffered, too. That was the oddest thing of all, but there was no doubt about it.

Dorothy looked after him that night as he climbed the stairs, and then turned to me with almost apologetic optimism. "He will settle down, won't he?" she said strenuously.

It was the first time we'd exchanged a word on the subject since the scene at breakfast a week or so before. I ought to have talked to her about him, I knew, but I was silenced by a double loyalty now. I couldn't confront Dorothy with the clinical aspects of her own pain, and I found that I could no more discuss Crispin with his mother than I could discuss his mother with him.

So I said: "Yes, give him time, and I'm sure he will," wondering all the time if he ever would.

"You see, I knew he'd like you. You're on good terms with him already. I only wish it was as easy as that for me!"

"I'm accepted up to a point," I said, "and that's all. I don't know myself yet where the limit's fixed, but I shall know if I ever step over it."

"I step over it every time I come into his sight," said Dorothy sadly. "Even if I really had slept with Tony, you wouldn't think I could have been damned like this for it, would you? I didn't think Bruce would teach him to hate me."

I didn't think so, either. Feeling as strongly about

morality as he did, he'd have been the last to talk about the mother's sins to the son.

" I'm sure that's not the trouble," I said firmly, willing to perjure my soul to lift even a little of the shadow from Dorothy's face. " I think he's just taking out his shock and resentment at his father's death on you as the nearest and most intimately connected person around. Oh, I suppose he did bear you a grudge because he felt you'd somehow let Bruce down, but after all these years that must be only an academic resentment. He's just making use of you as a scapegoat. Give him time ! He's young, he won't be able to help getting over it in the end."

" Do you really think so ? " she said.

She went up to bed with the ghost of a smile in the violet depths of her eyes, but it was still a sad smile.

I read late that night, and fell asleep over the book ; and it was the wind rising in the cool of the after-midnight hours that woke me up again. As I went sleepily and stiffly through the hall on my way to bed I heard the french door of the garden-room rattling, and revived just enough to realise that even in a brisk wind it rattled only when the bolt wasn't shot. Whereas I had quite certainly seen Hallam shoot the bolt home on his usual nightly round, well before midnight. Who could have unfastened it again at this hour ?

I went and tried it, to make sure. Both bolts were drawn back. Someone had presumably left the house by that route ; why else should anyone bother to open it ? And who was likely to be out for a walk in the small hours ? Nobody was likely ; only one person seemed a possibility.

Crispin had never invited me into his room, and apart from that one scuffle I'd never followed him there. But I went upstairs now, and opened the door gently upon his privacy. He wasn't in the bed ; it was still smooth and undisturbed. Well, he wasn't the first adolescent to retire

demurely to his room and then break out of the house on
ploys of his own at midnight. I remembered occasions
when I'd done as much myself. But for the right enjoyment of such excursions, as I remembered them, at least
one companion was needed, preferably more; and only
now did it dawn upon me how absolutely barren of com-
panions of his own age Crispin's life was. As he had sought
to strip all adults from him, so he had refrained from the
society of his contemporaries. He had literally not a friend
in the world. His isolation was so complete that to think of
him stealing out of the house at night on some illicit spree
was fantastic.

So my rôle was far from easy. True, I was nominally his
tutor, and had an almost parental responsibility for him,
but my terms of reference clashed somewhat with the tacit
terms of the relationship I'd struck up with him. No doubt
I ought to wait up for him and read the riot act; but my
acceptance of his obstinate reticence about his affairs, and
his acceptance of me in return for my forbearance, pre-
cluded my pressing him with questions if he chose not to
answer them.

If I'd known where to look for him I'd have gone out
after him; but lacking any indications to limit the field of
search, I made myself comfortable in a chair in the darkest
corner of the garden-room, and waited up for him. And a
long and anxious wait it seemed, especially after it had
suddenly occurred to me that he might, just might, be
intending never to come back at all. When you know
nothing whatever about a boy's motives, forecasting what
he'll do is utterly impossible.

However, I needn't have worried; he came back. Not
until nearly half past four in the morning, when the pre-
dawn radiance was already beginning to saturate the summer
darkness; but he came. I heard the soft crunching of the
gravel under light feet, then an interval of almost complete

silence as he crossed the terrace—he was evidently rubber-shod for his excursion—and finally the stealthy, gradual lifting of the latch under the pressure of his fingers. I edged along the wall until I stood near the door, screened by the long curtains, and as he slid through the doorway I dropped a hand on his shoulder.

The moment I touched him he jumped like a startled colt, and drew a great gasping breath that must have bruised his throat. Then without a wasted instant or another sound he turned and braced his arms against my chest, and hoisted a wicked knee at me, but I caught him by both arms and held him off. He fell quiet between my hands, and didn't struggle any more ; he knew now who I was. For one moment, I felt sure, he'd taken me for someone else, God knew who. I could hear the thudding hammer of his heart, and feel the deep, steadying breaths he drew down into him as he waited for the fright to pass. I wasn't supposed to know, but I knew.

I kept hold of him by one arm as I switched on the light. He stood glaring at me, and wouldn't say a word, but somewhere there lingered in him just enough of the school-boy to make him feel at a disadvantage, even if he refused to acknowledge it. He shook back his tumbled hair and straightened the neck of his sweater with a touch of bravado which I found disarming ; but he was watching me nar-rowly all the time, and waiting for the inevitable questions.

" Are you all right ? " I asked, purposely selecting one he wasn't expecting.

" Of course I am ! " he said, indignantly suppressing the last quaver of fright, and jerked at the arm I was holding. " You didn't have to jump out on me like that."

" You didn't *have* to come strolling in at half past four in the morning," I said reasonably. " If you do, you must expect strong reactions from me—I'm not of nocturnal habit myself. Now if you'd given me due notice——"

" I don't have to tell you what I intend to do," he said furiously. " I've fallen in with your school hours, haven't I ? What is it to you what I do with my own time ? "

" That's a point that could do with some clearing up, certainly. Well, suppose we consult your mother, and get my terms of reference properly formulated, shall we ? Then we shall both know where we stand." And I towed him a couple of paces towards the door into the hall, I admit very basely, since I had not the least intention that Dorothy should ever hear a word about this little encounter. He stiffened and dug in his heels indignantly, clutching at my arm with his free hand.

" *No* ! *Please*, no ! You *mus:n't* tell her ! Oh, hell ! " he said wildly, " why can't you leave me alone, or fight me fairly ? I don't know where I am with you. The other bloke at least *behaved* like a beak——"

" All right," I agreed, halting obligingly, " let's start again according to the rules. Account for yourself ! Where have you been ? " I held him facing me, and shook him to emphasise the gravity of the question. But still he wasn't happy ; maybe I failed to stop short of caricature.

" Oh, damn you ! Out ! " he said flatly, despairing of achieving anything creditable or dignified.

" Out, where ? And what have you been up to ? "

" I've been meeting a girl, if you really want to know," he said, with a flash of malicious insolence, and turned scarlet as I laughed. I hadn't meant to, but the thought of this haggard, single-minded young recluse indulging in dalliance was as funny as it was pathetic.

" I'm sorry, Crispin, but *really* ! If I haven't deserved the truth, at least I've earned a better lie than that."

" It's all you'll get," he said fiercely, his chin shaking with frustration and rage. " Look, if you've got to come the tutor, all right, for God's sake let's get it over. Give me some extra work to do, or detention, or thrash me, or what ever the damnfool drill is—I won't kick! Only *leave my mother out of it!* And just *don't jaw!* I'm too tired."

I propelled him gently backwards into a chair, and stood over him. " Now, look here, Crispin," I said seriously, " you know and I know that you've got something on your mind, something that's worrying you sick. You know and I know that you didn't sneak out of the house to-night for fun, or for mischief, either. You don't want me to pry, and I've no wish to. I'm not asking questions. I give you my word I won't. I'm just begging you to think it over carefully, and see if you can't share it with me."

He sat turning his head helplessly from side to side, trying to evade me. He said in a lost voice : " I wish I——" and then pulled himself together with a shudder, and burst out bitterly : " I wish you'd go away and leave me alone! I wish you'd never come here! "

It was useless pushing him any further. I hoisted him resignedly out of the chair, and propelled him gently into the hall, starting him up the stairs with a slap between the shoulders. " Get off to bed now. No, don't be an ass, your mother'll never hear anything from me about your goings-on. Go and sleep it off! Shall I bring your breakfast up to you for once ? "

Without turning his head he said : " No," rather stiffly ; and two stairs higher, in a small and brittle voice : " Thank you ! "

CHAPTER V

DERMOT CRANE arrived in a small Austin, shortly before lunch the next day. I had rather supposed that Crispin would absent himself from the welcoming committee on the doorstep, but he was firmly, almost menacingly present, somewhat hollow-eyed from his night on the tiles, but stonily composed. When Dorothy looked round for him, half commanding and half appealing for his co-operation, he came forward with his best social manner, cool, bright and boyish, the dutiful youngster being polite to his elders. It didn't commit him to anything, it was a manner as well adapted to enemies as to friends.

Crane was a big man, round about forty years old but exceedingly trim and athletic, and decidedly good-looking. His was also a cool style, except towards Dorothy. He looked Crispin over with a quick, assessing eye, and I think would have shaken hands with him, if Crispin hadn't kept his distance, and made his arrogantly courtly little bow from the top of the steps. Watching them, I reflected that these two must know each other very well; they had been at least two months in the party at Pirithoön, and must have established some sort of relationship, maybe warmer than this meeting indicated, maybe colder, but certainly more casual and relaxed.

" Hallo, Crispin, how are you ? Nice to see you again ! "

Crispin said : " I'm glad to see you, too, Dermot." And he meant it, for he said it with emphatic deliberation. But the careful distinction he had made between his own expression of pleasure and Dermot's was something I didn't miss. I was beginning to be expert in Crispin's subtleties.

I helped the visitor to unload his belongings from the

car, and we installed him in one of the big front bedrooms. He knew the house, it seemed, from one visit made during Bruce's lifetime, and he refreshed his memory as we climbed the stairs and crossed the lordly Georgian landing.

" That's the room Bruce always used, I remember. He liked the view over the town."

" Crispin has it now." said Dorothy, pushing open the door for a moment upon that curiously impersonal and temporary-looking apartment. " He adored his father— I wanted him to have everything that was Bruce's."

" How does he seem ? " asked Crane, as she closed the door again. " Is he settling down ? Getting used to doing without Bruce ? He was always a sensible kid, older than his age—at least when he was concerned with anything serious. I hoped he'd be all right once you got him home. He looks well. How's he behaving ? "

Dorothy was very willing to talk about her son and his difficulties of adjustment. I left them to it, and presently she came down looking eased and comforted, and I knew she'd poured out the whole story. There was no reason why she shouldn't, after all. Crane was an intimate of all the parties concerned, and knew, as I did not, all the details of the tragedy at Pirithoön. All the same, I felt a twinge of jealousy at the thought that she should confide in him as she'd confided in me.

The telephone rang just as she came down the stairs. She lifted the receiver abstractedly, expecting some casual routine call, and the next moment flashed into astonishment and pleasure.

" David ! What a coincidence ! Where are you ? Yes, of course come to us, we shall be very angry if you don't. No, of course you won't be ! Do you know who's here ? Dermot Crane ! Yes, he just arrived about an hour ago, for the week-end. Yes, do come, David, he'll be delighted to see you, and so shall we. Take a bus, it will drop you

outside our gate. Ask for the Lawns. Yes, of course I'm
sure ! I look forward to seeing you again."

When she laid the receiver back in its cradle, Crispin was
standing in the doorway of the library, looking at her with
eyes dark-circled and intent. " David ? Did you say
David ? "

" Yes, isn't it odd that he should turn up, too ? "

" David Keyes ? "

" What other David do we know ? He was on his way
to Cornwall for a touring week-end, but his motor-bike's
broken down, and he can't get it repaired until to-morrow.
He's stranded in Wells, so he rang up to ask if he could come
and see us, as he's so near. I told him to come and spend
the week-end here."

" Quite a reunion party this is going to be, isn't it ? "
said Crispin.

" Dermot will be pleased," said Dorothy. " I must go
and tell Mrs. Hallam to get another room ready." And she
was gone, and I was left considering Crispin's blank front
as he stared reflectively after her.

" This David was in your father's party at Pirithoön,
too ? "

" The last month he was. He's doing some post-graduate
job at London University. He was in Greece on his own
until he asked Bruce if he could come and join us on the
dig."

Hazarding a judgment for which I had very little evidence,
I said : " This is something you weren't expecting."

" No," he agreed, giving me a long look, " I wasn't
expecting both of them." And he turned and walked out
into the garden, and didn't come back until I went to call
him in to lunch.

It seemed to me that throughout the meal Crane paid
close attention to every move that Crispin made, and every
word he said, and was doing his level best to draw the boy

out, and establish a ground of communication with him—or perhaps, more accurately, re-establish a ground they'd once possessed. And Crispin, for his part, wore throughout a face of bright, hard, social interest, so dutiful that it had at times a quality of self-satire which was profoundly disturbing, at least to me. He talked readily, and said remarkably little. And all the time he watched them. It was natural enough that Dorothy should have seated Dermot beside her, and their behaviour was unexceptionable, indeed they devoted themselves by mutual consent to Crispin rather than to each other. If they made it a little too easy to guess that they had had a long talk about him in private, that was their only indiscretion. Yet his eyes as he watched them were black and quite opaque with the distance he had set between himself and them.

And suddenly, blindingly, I understood. It wasn't that Crispin had too little affection for his mother. Nothing so simple. It was rather that he had too much. He resented every man who came near her, as he resented being sent away from her himself. It accounted for the fate of my predecessor, it accounted for his ambivalent attitude to me, though as a person he had accepted me. Even his nocturnal jaunt seemed now no more than a hysterical act of protest against the coming of Dermot Crane. No one must touch her, no one must admire her, no one must share her attention with him.

I ought to have foreseen the possibility. It was only too natural, seeing he had met her for the first time, as it were, when he was fifteen, and exceptionally mature for his years, and she was a dazzlingly attractive woman.

And that being that, we were all of us in a sufficiently difficult and delicate spot, but once recognised, it could be handled. It would take a lot of tact and patience and practical, low cunning, but it could be done. I heaved a sigh of relief, because Crispin had lost in a moment all his mystery and menace, and been scaled down into a figure of pathos more in keeping with his age.

I ought to have known better ! Never in my life have I been as sure as that of my own rightness, without being proved dead wrong the next moment, before I even had time to hedge !

CHAPTER VI

DAVID KEYES turned up half-way through the afternoon, lugging a week-end bag, and striding up the drive with eagerness and energy enough for ten men. He was burned to an Indian red by the same archæological sun, presumably, which had tanned Dermot Crane to a metallic bronze, and his hair was deep chestnut, and looked like a slow fire that had started in his forehead. His age was anybody's guess, students and graduates being alike so undateable. I put him at about twenty-eight, but I could have been a few years out in either direction. Shorter than Crane, and by no means so striking, but a pleasant person to look at, and blessed with the open countenance women usually take to. I looked sideways at Crispin, who hadn't expected both of them. There was no reading anything more profound than his social duty in his face, or in his voice as he said : " Hallo, David ! How are you ? "

" Hot and dirty," said David heartily, taking a step back from him with oily hands raised, and thus neatly obviating any awkwardness there might have been about shaking hands. " Don't touch me until I've had a wash. I've been trying to make the old bike go, but it beat me in the end." And he turned cheerfully to meet Dorothy, as she came out into the hall, with an enthusiastic gesture of his arms which was almost an embrace, and soiled palms displayed to ward her off. "Mrs. Almond, this is awfully kind of you! I'm afraid I must be putting you out terribly, dropping on you without warning like this."

She smiled at him, a nice, easy smile she wouldn't have bestowed, I thought, on anybody who disturbed her peace of mind to any noticeable extent. But how Crispin read it there was no knowing.

"Don't be silly, David, you know you're always welcome. I expected you to come and see us long ago."

"I didn't like to presume too much on such a short acquaintance. And I knew you'd have your hands full, with all Bruce's affairs." Especially Crispin, I thought, all the more because he didn't say it; and I was pretty sure that Crispin was thinking it too.

"Have you had any lunch?"

"Sandwiches. I ate them before I pushed the damned bike the last half mile to the garage."

"Poor David! I must see to it that the tea's substantial. Dermot's somewhere in the garden, he can't have seen you arrive. Yes, do go and change into something cool and comfortable. By the time you're ready tea shall be ready too."

I took him up to his room, and he talked every step of the way, and seemed inclined to go on talking indefinitely, about Bruce and Pirithoön, about what a marvellous chap he'd been, and what a wonderful woman Dorothy was, and what a fine kid Crispin was, until I wondered if anyone could really be as extrovert as all that. And then he suddenly asked: "How do we stand? Does one talk about what happened in the Peloponnese? In front of the boy, I mean?"

"It's an experiment we haven't tried," I said, "since I've been in the house."

"It might be a mistake to avoid it too rigorously," he said, with more shrewdness than I'd been giving him credit for. " He was in a state of stone-cold shock when she took him away from Greece, you know. Like a walking icicle. Lucid, intelligent, aware, confiding in nobody. But he can't go on all through his life in a state of post-shock coddling, with everybody conspiring to create an artificial world for him, in which Bruce didn't die, but just quietly and decorously vanished. Mrs. Almond was only too plainly nervous of him from the start. I thought she was making a mistake."

" Try opening a window," I suggested. " I don't suppose the subject can be avoided, in any case, when you and Crane get together. Personally I haven't been in a position to introduce the subject. I know practically nothing about it, not even where Pirithoön is."

" It's in the hills of the Argolid, not far from Mycenæ. There are traces of the same sort of monumental city walls there, but on nothing like such a big scale. Bruce was cutting into the mound outside the walls, he was convinced there were tombs there—Homeric tombs. To be honest— and you mustn't think I'm knocking Bruce now he's dead, this was common knowledge about him, anybody'll tell you —any tomb Bruce found in that locality would have been automatically a Homeric tomb, and any bit of a gold pectoral or pendant would have been a relic of Cassandra's jewellery, or Clytemnestra's. He was like that. There'd been a few finds, some pottery, a few trinkets, nothing very much. But we'd just uncovered what did look like being the entrance of a fairly large chamber. You know the pattern, a sloping passageway built of cut stones, and a lintelled doorway, and that triangular slab above the lintel, something like at Mycenæ, only not nearly so massive. It was early days to tell, we'd only uncovered the upper part of the doorway, and lifted out parts of the triangular entablature, which was broken. Personally I wasn't at all sure about dating it, but Bruce was certain it was round about 1200 B.C. Dermot had his doubts, too, I know. But Bruce's gang would go on with him even when they didn't really believe he was on to anything, or trust his judgment. He was that sort of person. You couldn't even disappoint him by saying what you thought, except in the mildest terms. It would have been like hitting a baby."

Well, that squared with everything Dorothy had said about him. It seemed the charm worked on men too.

" But the kids were shamelessly frank about *their* scepticism," said David with a grin.

" The kids ? "

" Crispin and Nikos, the foreman's boy. They made no secret of it, they guyed the whole affair. Of course, they'd probably have been blasé about antiquities, in any case, but they didn't seriously believe in Bruce's hunches, or his dating. There was a fearful row over one leg-pull they worked on him."

" Mrs. Almond," I said, " cherishes the illusion that Crispin adored his father."

This fellow wasn't by any means as simple as I'd thought him. " Oh, he did," he assured me, surprised. " It's no illusion, he did adore him. But he thought he was quite crazy." On reflection this seemed to me, as it evidently did to him, an entirely feasible attitude.

" How did Bruce's accident happen ? " I asked. " All I've heard about it is that a stone lintel fell on him and crushed him. Was that the lintel of this tomb he was excavating ? "

" Oh, no, it happened up above, on the hill. It was the gateway to the little Acropolis that collapsed on him. The citadel is very ruinous, there's hardly anything left to be seen except the gateway and a few relics of the wall. And the gate was pretty precarious, we knew that, though I was rather surprised that it gave the way it did. It was late one night it happened, and nobody saw it, there was nobody with him at the time, we were all in bed, and most of us asleep. We lived in several of the village houses, and the inn, all except Bruce and the boy and Crane, who'd managed to rent a very small villa nearly on the site. I don't think it was anything new for Bruce to be wandering about Pirithoön at night by himself. He was a romantic, he'd be peopling the place with Homeric royalties ten feet high. Anyhow, Crane heard the fall, and got up and went to investigate, and found Bruce dead under the stone, and Crispin kneeling by him. Smashed from hips to shoulders, the thing was diagonally across him. Crane said at the time he thought, when he woke up, that a minor earthquake shock had shaken the place, but then he realised it had been too clearly one single impact. They felt the vibration down in the village."

"What happened? Did the police have to come into it?"

"Oh, yes, they took over at once. But it was pretty clear how it had happened, everybody knew the place wasn't too safe. Mrs. Almond came rushing out from Athens at once, and claimed the boy. He was in a queer state, too quiet and self-contained by half. The important thing seemed to be to get him out of there. She left Crane to take care of everything at Pirithoön, and went back to Athens with Crispin by car the very next day. We buried Bruce in the village. It seemed to be what he would have liked."

"And the dig?"

He grinned. "Without Bruce there wasn't any dig. It was his money, he could throw it away on an unpromising site if he liked. But nobody else believed in it enough or had enough spare cash, to take it over, even if the authorities would have given permission, and I doubt if they would have been very keen. One tragedy like that was enough. No, Bruce's death effectively closed the dig. I came away soon afterwards. Crane stayed on to tidy up the site and clear up all Bruce's affairs locally. The tomb and the open passage were left just as they were."

I thought of Bruce Almond, or what was left of him, buried there in the grey-green, tumbled hills of the Argolid which I knew only from photographs. It seemed a pointless way to die in one's prime, and death untimely ought at least to have point. Especially there in the monstrous shadow of Mycenæ, where the bloodiest cruelties fell into place as essentials in a pattern of enormous and significant grandeur and beauty. It didn't seem as if that could be all the story.

I went down and left him to clean himself up in peace. He took his time about it. It must have been three-quarters of an hour before he came out and joined us in the garden, looking cool and scrubbed, and rather juvenile, in slacks and an open-necked shirt, and full of apologies for being so long.

It was a beautiful, hot afternoon, and with our circle of deck-chairs, and tea on the lawn, we looked like an idyll of the English summer. And even our dialogue might have been lifted almost intact from some country-house comedy, so innocuous it was, and so unreal. Nobody opened a window, after all. Pirithoön was mentioned, but only in connection with the few pieces of pottery and glaze which had been found there, in the course of a blameless interlude of archæological shop. Apart from being ordinarily attentive, and making the appropriate noises at intervals, I took no part at all. I was much more interested in watching them all, and waiting for the unguarded glance, the dropped word, the secret intonation that would make sense of the whole obscure tangle. But my waiting wasn't rewarded.

Not, at least, until after tea, when Dorothy led her visitors away to look at the gardens and the shrubberies, and I went indoors to fetch some cigarettes. Crispin looked up at me from his deck-chair as I rose, and asked unexpectedly:

"Are you going upstairs ? Would you mind bringing my camera down ? It's in the top of my desk." That was the large old desk which had once been Bruce's property.

It was the first time he'd ever made such a request of me, and better still, he did it without thought or hesitation. And suddenly I had the impression that I was the first person he'd ever approached without care or calculation since Bruce died. Maybe it was only a lapse on his part, and when he recollected himself he'd recoil into his tower.

Instead, something very different happened. I'd barely reached the edge of the lawn when he called after me, and came running. His face was flushed ; he had indeed recollected himself.

"I forgot," he said, "the desk's locked. You'll need these." And he held out to me the small key-ring which had also belonged to Bruce, and put it into my hand with a movement suddenly almost awkward.

There was nothing uncalculated about this move ; that was the beauty of it. It was a ritual gesture, marking another stage in our relationship ; he turned over his treasures to me with a heightened colour, and withdrew again quickly, before I could say a word. And I felt honoured and burdened in equal measure, because Crispin's confidences, when they came, weren't going to be easy to carry.

The desk was mahogany, and massive, with a top that folded back when it was unlocked. I slid the key into the lock, and it turned so far, and then grated and stuck. I tried coaxing it, feeling my way gingerly into the wards, but it wouldn't turn until I exerted a fair amount of force, and then it ground protestingly past the point of obstruction, and the flap opened.

There was something wrong about that lock. The desk was so beautifully kept that such a faulty action in the most important part of it made no sense. I looked carefully at the wood round the keyhole, and there were a few fine scratches that certainly had no business there. They were fresh, and they spoke for themselves very clearly.

I looked carefully at the interior of the desk, but it appeared scrupulously tidy and untouched. Whoever had been looking for whatever he'd been looking for had had no occasion to move anything within ; evidently he could see at a glance whether the thing sought for was or was not there.

I investigated no further, there was no need. I went down to Crispin, who was waiting for me at the edge of the lawn, his eyes fixed thoughtfully on the three people walking along the path in the distance.

" Come upstairs," I said, " there's something I want you to see."

He gave me a brilliant, intent stare, and came at once, without a single question. I think he'd been waiting for something to happen, without knowing in the least what to expect. He turned the key as I told him to turn it, and when it grated to a stop in the strained wards his face sharpened and his eyes grew dark and wary. He, too, looked at the wood round the keyhole. He understood very well.

Without a word he turned from the brief glance he had cast at the contents of the desk-top, and began to open the drawers, one by one. Then he sat down on the bed, and let his hands fall on his knees, and looked steadily at me.

" Whatever it may be," I said. " I trust it wasn't there to be found ? "

" No," he said in a low voice. " It wasn't there."

" Without wishing to intrude in your affairs," I said, " I must wonder, being human, which of our visitors has been going through your belongings so carefully. This morning Crane was upstairs alone for some considerable time. But so was Keyes this afternoon, before tea. Any idea which of them picked the lock of your desk ? "

" No," said Crispin in the same tone, " I only wish I had."

" You were expecting one of them, and only one, to turn up here. And that would have solved something for you. But now that they're both in the house you're no nearer knowing—whatever it was you wanted to know."

He didn't say anything this time, only sat there with his clenched fists pushing down hard against his thighs, and stared at me with his dark, considering, agonised eyes, his face quite still. He didn't know what to do about me. I knew too much, or not enough ; and he couldn't get rid of me, and in his heart he wanted me, not even moderately, but desperately. He wanted me so that he needn't be entirely alone any longer.

" If you want me to shut up and go away," I said, " you've only to say so. I'll still be on hand whenever you need me."

" No," he said, " I can't go on taking things from you and not giving you anything in return. No—please don't go, Evelyn ! "

He was so convulsed with the effort of getting over his own fence that I don't think he noticed he'd used my name. But I noticed, all right. It was the first time, and it underlined my conviction that something had changed for ever in our relationship.

" You won't go right away and leave me to manage things by myself," he said, dragging the words up by the roots out of the middle of his being, " so I must tell you—at least as much as you need to know to be able to look after yourself. I wanted you to go, I wanted nobody else to be involved but me. It was my fight. I began it, I engineered it, I didn't want it to touch anyone else. But you wouldn't go, and now it's too late, anyhow."

" I'm not complaining," I said, " and you needn't feel at all responsible for me. As you say, you gave me every chance, and I didn't take it. It's entirely up to you how much you tell me."

" You're right, of course," he said, " either David Keyes or Dermot Crane broke into the desk. Searched the whole room, probably. It doesn't matter, what he wanted isn't here. Only, as you said, the hell of it is we're no nearer knowing which of them it is."

He drew a deep breath, and twisted uneasily where he sat. He'd lost the habit of confiding in anyone, and it didn't come back easily. Since it was obvious that he wanted to tell me, I helped him out with a question.

" What was it he was looking for ? "

Crispin looked up at me suddenly with a brilliant and bitter smile. " What is it they're always looking for ? He was looking for gold ! "

CHAPTER VII

IT WASN'T A JOKE, he didn't make jokes about this enormous burden he carried on his shoulders, it was too real for that. The most he permitted himself was this sidelong, satirical glance, as if he stepped back to get an outsider's look at something which was normally so close to him that he couldn't see it at all without a mirror.

" Gold from Pirithoön," I said. Not asking him, just telling myself so much aloud ; for it had to be that.

Crispin said : " Yes—' near the ruins of Mycenæ, rich in gold.' They must have looted it from all over the Eastern Mediterranean, I suppose, to have so much. They stuck gold bosses on the walls of their tombs, and gold leaf on the faces of their dead, and gold armlets on their arms, and gold pectorals on their breasts. All their history was blood and gold. Why should it be different now ? "

As yet he was talking to himself, not to me. He drew up his knees, and wound his arms round them, and rocked gently on the edge of the bed. I waited. Presently he would begin to talk to me, and then his utterance would be clear enough.

" It was Nikos and I who began it all. Nikos was Stavros's son. He was two years younger than me, and we spent most of our time together. We were so bored with trivial antiquities that we were rather looking for mischief. Bruce had found one or two things, and sent them off to Athens, because Professor Barclay was there—you know, Professor John Barclay ?—on some research job at the university, and of course his opinion is the best you could have on Mycenæn culture. Anything we turned up was whipped off to him, though he was pretty damping in his response most of the time. Well, Bruce had dug out a stone passageway going gently downwards into the mounds outside the walls, and he was convinced he was on to another beehive tomb like the great ones at Mycenæ. They'd just dug their way to what did seem to be the entrance to a chamber, but the stonework was a good deal crumbled, and the big slab sealing the upper part of the doorway was broken. They hadn't got through the rubble deep enough to make an entrance into the chamber, but the broken stone did leave a very small gap at the top. Not enough for a man to get through, but enough for a boy.

" During the day Nikos and I usually kept off the site, but one night we happened to go there, and there was nobody to shoo us away, and there was the chink among the slabs of stone. We thought we might as well have a look inside. We fetched a rope, because it looked as if whoever went in would have to let himself down quite a way to the floor of the chamber. It was Nikos who went, because he was lighter and smaller than I was. He climbed down out of sight while I kept watch and managed the rope. He had a torch, of course, but as it turned out he got scared once he was down there inside, and didn't dare go more than a few yards into the passageway. Then he yelled to me that he was coming out, and I helped to pull him up as he climbed out."

It was odd how Crispin had relapsed into boys' language as he described the last incident of his childhood, that childhood he had put on and taken off at will through the easy years with Bruce. He was with Nikos again, half-scared and half-audacious in the darkness of a spring night over the unpromising rubbish-heap of stonework which might or might not be a tomb. I could almost hear them smothering their giggles over the follies of their elders. He must have been about twelve years old then, not fifteen.

" He said part of the masonry had caved in, and there was a lot of rubble lying about down there, but there was a way through into an inner chamber, all right. He didn't see anything of it except the doorway, because then he got windy, and couldn't get out again fast enough. But he didn't come out empty-handed. He brought out a crumpled piece of thin, soft metal, he said he'd kicked it and heard it ring as he backed towards the rope again, so he put it inside his coat. I think probably it got even more bent and battered on the way up. It was shaped something like a stylised drawing of a bird—look, here a thin, tapered body in the middle, and on either side a wing-shaped piece coming down to a point, like this, and all across the top a solid band about three inches wide right across body and wings."

His slim forefinger drew carefully upon the quilt, shaping a band about a foot long, with the two wings and the central thin dagger-shape depending from it. " That was after we'd flattened it out neatly. At first it was half curled round, like the seal off a cigar band, and bent and crumpled, too, here and there. It was a dark colour like the colour of earth, but where we bent it back into shape it made very thin bright streaks in it, like a pattern. And if you drew on it with something not sharp enough to scratch, but just to indent it, like a thumb-nail, it made the same sort of brighter chasings.

" We didn't think much about it. It didn't look much, and we didn't believe in the site, anyhow, and didn't expect anything from it. But we were spoiling for something to do, so we took this thing away with us, and flattened it out very carefully, and chased a few nice appropriate designs on it, with mazes and spirals and all the usual Mycenæn things, and altogether we made it look a fairly credible sort of pectoral ornament. And then I took it to Bruce, and told him where we'd found it. Dead-pan, thirsting for information and full of hope.

" He swallowed it whole. I knew he would. He was such an optimist he couldn't help seeing what he wanted to see. He called in Dermot and David to help him gloat over it, and after he'd done building about five centuries of history on it he gave it to Dermot to lock up in the safe. He could hardly bear to let it out of his sight, he was so wild with excitement about it. And Nikos and I had to get well out of earshot to be able to laugh properly, so we went down to the village for the rest of the day. Otherwise we should have given the show away.

" But the next day, when we got up, we had an awful shock, because Bruce had packed the thing up and sent David off to Athens with it in person, to Professor Barclay, to get his opinion on it. We hadn't intended the joke to go as far as that, and if only poor old Bruce hadn't been in such a feverish hurry to start the thing on its way before daybreak we could have stopped him from making a fool of himself. *We* made a fool of him, and laughed about his enthusiasm, and all that, but we didn't like anybody else doing the same. As long as it was in the family, so to speak, it was all right. But especially not expérts ! Bruce was the natural butt of the experts, anyhow, we hated to think we'd given them some ammunition to fire at him. But it was too

late, we couldn't do anything about it. David was already
on his way.

" You know how it is, when something like that is hanging
over you," said Crispin, for once looking up at me almost
appealingly. " You try to convince yourself that it won't
turn out the bad way, that by some fluke the disaster won't
materialise. But it always does. This did. Professor Barclay
didn't reply for a couple of days, and David had nothing to
report, because he'd only delivered it, the professor wasn't
there to examine it on the spot. But then there was a letter
from Athens at breakfast, and I knew we'd had it. Not
that Bruce said anything to me then, of course, but his face
was enough. And when he showed the letter to the others
on the site I stuck close enough to get the gist of it. I had
to, I was responsible. At least, I can't remember for certain
whether the bright idea was mine or Nikos's, but I think it
was mine, and anyhow, we were both in it, up to the neck."

I wasn't entirely impressed by this sense of guilty responsibility towards a father who ought surely to have known
twice as much about any relics found on the soil of Pirithoön
as those two boys could be expected to know. I said as
much, but Crispin shook his head emphatically. He knew
his own father, if any boy ever did.

" Oh, no, because Bruce was so innocent. You can't
understand, you didn't know him. He was so innocent he
was dangerous. He was bound to be at the world's mercy
all his life, there wasn't a confidence trick you couldn't have
worked on him."

" All right," I said, " so you felt responsible for him.
What was it you'd let him in for ? "

" Professor Barclay wrote that someone was hoaxing him
with a botched forgery, and a brand-new forgery at that,
and that he was sending back the supposed pectoral under
separate cover. He said he didn't feel it was necessary to
register it, as it was valueless."

" Cutting," I commented, " but coming from an expert whose time had been wasted, I suppose it was justifiable. Well, and what did you do about it ? "

" What could we do ? Went and owned up, told them the whole story. There was an awful row. Stavros just took Nikos by the scruff of the neck and laid into him with his belt on the spot, and so of course Bruce couldn't in justice do less by me. The only time he ever did ! But he couldn't very well let me off with a lecture, when Nikos was getting a hiding—especially as I was the principal in the affair."

" I trust he made a good job of it ? " I said.

A fleeting grin passed over Crispin's cloudy face, and faded again instantly into the darkness of his memories. " He rather overdid it, as a matter of fact," he said tolerantly. " He was nervous, not being used to it, and he had to screw himself up to such a pitch of resolution that it ran away with him."

" I hope it did you good ! "

The smile showed again for a moment ; but it was as if he smiled at something which had happened to somebody else, perhaps in a book. The grim composure to which his face always returned was the present reality.

" It did, but not the way you mean. I was feeling so bad about the whole thing by then that it was a real relief to work off a bit of my debts, even that way. Actually he needn't have put himself out, I should have paid anyhow. Stavros always took care of both of us, he took it for granted any scrape Nikos was in I was in, too. But of course Bruce didn't know that, he mightn't have liked it. He might even have felt badly enough about it to fire Stavros, if he'd known. And we. couldn't have got on without Stavros, either of us. He was the one really practical person on the dig."

My mental picture of the spoiled, indulged, precocious,

socially accomplished boy of Pirithoön was changing shape every moment. He seemed to turn to me alternate profiles, one a child, the other a man, as he talked. In an adolescent boy such unco-ordinated glimpses are not, perhaps, so strange, but somehow in him the gulf between the two seemed impassably wide, as though they never would meet and marry, as though he made no effort to reconcile them because he already knew that it was pointless, that for that fused image which is the achievement of manhood there was never, in his case, going to be any future. And he worried me as he'd never worried me before. That was how I first became aware that I'd grown unwisely fond of him. How it had happened I don't know. I know it hadn't been difficult.

" Well, so I suppose the row blew over," I said. " What next ? "

" Next," said Crispin, looking through me into a bleak distance, " I woke up in the middle of the night—that same night—and thought I'd been awakened by thunder. Only there wasn't any more thunder, and the sky was clear. It was after midnight, I think about twenty minutes past the hour. I was frightened, though I don't know why. I wondered that Bruce hadn't been startled awake, too, and I looked in his room, and he wasn't in the bed. Wasn't there, hadn't been there. We lived in a little villa very near the site, above the village, just Bruce and I, with Dermot Crane, and Stavros's wife looked after the house for us. I didn't think of looking for Dermot, I just ran out in my pyjamas to find out what had happened. By then I knew that something had. There was nobody moving about the site. I went uphill, towards the citadel. It seemed to me then—though it hadn't at first—that that was where the crash had come from. The night wasn't dark, the sky had a sort of luminosity, even without a moon. I could see where the gateway of the citadel ought to have stood out against that sky, and didn't.

" I was running when I realised that it was gone. And when I stopped dead, there it was on the ground, driven into the soil at one corner, and from under it stuck out a head and neck, and one shoulder and arm, and the rest of whoever it was was underneath the stone. I hadn't got a torch. I knelt down by the head. I touched him. When you know somebody well enough just a shape, hardly seen at all, is recognisable. I saw that it was Bruce. His eyes were open, they showed faintly luminous, too. He was dead."

I waited, and his face was motionless and quite composed. He paused only to assemble within his memory's inexorable eye the details of the hour. He did not want to forget anything, or misvalue anything. He wanted the act, the reality of it in full, to remain as clear and revealing as the air of Greece, as glitteringly cruel as truth, as satisfying as truth.

" I heard people running," he continued, his head reared as if he were listening to distant footsteps at that moment. " One person near, others farther away. Somewhere in the distance I heard voices. I didn't feel anything that I can remember, I was too concerned just with grasping things. Then somebody came running behind me, and almost fell over me, and it was Dermot. He caught hold of me by the shoulders and began to say something, but I don't know what it was. Then he peered down and saw Bruce. And then there were other people coming, David, and Stavros, and some of the men from the village. Dermot hoisted me up from the ground, and tried to lead me away from the place, back towards the house, and when I stood still and didn't want to go, he picked me up and carried me. And I let him then, because it made no difference. There was nothing to be learned there but what I'd learned already. Everything stopped mattering, it might as well have stopped happening. I suppose it was shock. I don't know, I've no experience, but I suppose it was a state of shock. I didn't make trouble. They wanted me to go back to bed, and I went. A doctor came, and gave me a sedative, and I took it. I did whatever they told me to do. It seemed the best and easiest thing to humour them. They said go to sleep, and I went to sleep.

" I woke up quite suddenly, when it wasn't yet light but wasn't any longer quite dark, and when I looked at my watch it was about a quarter to four. I woke up very clear-headed, and remembering everything, and I suppose it was the first time I really knew that Bruce was dead. It was perfectly still and quiet in the house, there didn't seem to be anybody there but me. I suppose the police were already up on the citadel, though goodness knows there wasn't much they could do. I got up out of bed, and went into Bruce's room, I don't know why, just wanting something of his to see and touch, I think. It seemed as though I had to reassure myself quickly that he had been there, before all the feel of him had worn off things. I was frightened of forgetting. That's terrible, isn't it ? Not of forgetting *him*, but of forgetting just what his voice sounded like, and the way he looked. I didn't want the outlines to get vague and soft. I'd rather they were painful.

" I wandered round his room holding on to things, feeling his coat in the wardrobe, and his books on the shelves. And then I went downstairs into his office, and sat in the chair at his desk, and picked up his pens, and the letters he'd left shut into the blotter.

" He hadn't left much of a lifework, you see, for people to remember. I'd have given anything if only there'd been some big wonderful thing he'd found, something going back deep into the marvellous, like Troy. Even if the experts could still say it was only a fluke ! Even if they were *right* to say it ! And there wasn't anything. Only a small parcel on the desk from the previous afternoon's post, a parcel he hadn't bothered to open because, of course, he knew what was in it, and he was too hurt and angry to want to look at it again. I knew what it was, too, by the shape. It was our miserable little faked pectoral ornament. And it was the last thing I'd ever wanted to do to him, but I had, and it *had* been the last thing I'd ever done to him, and I could never make up for it.

" And then I opened the parcel. I don't know why. I so easily might not have done it, because it was no comfort to me to look at the thing, either. But I did, I suppose just because I was sitting there, and it was something for my hands to do. I opened it, and looked at it, and there it was, that bird shape with the octopus-like squiggles chased into it.

" Only it wasn't the same one ! It looked the same, it looked line for line the same. But it wasn't."

" How could you be so sure of that ? " I asked, startled.

" It didn't handle quite like the other. Not only the weight, but the texture, too. It felt harder and colder, and somehow not quite right. I held it in my hands, just as I'd held the other, and it didn't feel familiar to me. I had no conviction of ever having touched it before. And once I had that queer feeling about it, I could even see tiny differences in the lines of the decoration, and in the edges of the wings. It was a copy of ours, but it wasn't ours."

" Are you absolutely sure of that ? " I insisted, for this was so odd a turn in his story that it made no sense, and fitted in with nothing that had gone before. " You're sure you didn't persuade yourself of all these differences simply because you were subconsciously looking for a distraction, anything to get your mind off what had happened ? "

" Neither consciously nor subconsciously did I want my mind taken off what had happened," he said, with a brief, arrogant glare at me across the room. " And I didn't persuade myself of anything. I was quite sure then, and I'm quite sure now, that the pectoral that was sent back from

Athens was a different one from the one we'd used to pull Bruce's leg. I'm not imagining things, Evelyn, I *know*."

" Very well, go on. What did you do about it ? "

" I wrapped it up again, loosely, not pretending it hadn't been opened, only rather leaving it as if Bruce had opened it and then pushed it on one side."

" You didn't say anything to anyone about it ? "

" No. I had to think before I spoke. Before I spoke to anyone. David came in and found me there in the office, and shooed me back to bed, and then I really did sleep. I suppose I was exhausted just from nervous reaction, because I didn't wake up again until almost noon, and they all took good care not to wake me. They were probably glad to have me out of their way, there was a lot of going and coming, and police still running about the site, and heavy equipment to lift the stone. And half-way through the afternoon my mother arrived in a hired car from Athens, and after that she was with me every moment, hedging me away from what was happening on the citadel, never letting me out of her sight. You can do the journey from Athens to Pirithoön and back in one day, with a rush, but she had to stay overnight and leave with me next day, because of the formalities. Everybody was being most accommodating and considerate to us, I gathered, on account of our bereavement. They made everything easy, they even bent a few regulations for us. When she told them she wanted to take me back to the capital with her next day, and to England as soon as it could be arranged, they went to a lot of trouble to clear the obstacles out of her way. My mother has that effect on most men—even officials," he said with a tight little smile.

If he expected protest or comment, he didn't get them ; I wasn't prepared to discuss Dorothy with her son. And in a moment he resumed in a gentler tone : " She was very kind to me, I know, only she overdid it, and treated me like a child, who has to be protected from knowing anything about the facts of life, and in particular about the facts of death. She hardly took her eyes off me all the rest of that day, until she thought I was fast asleep in my bed at night. But I wasn't. I still had all that thinking to do, and I hadn't got anywhere with it yet. I kept on and on asking myself : Why should our fake be removed and another one put in its place ? And there could be only one answer : Because somebody wanted to keep the original without anyone else knowing anything about it. And then up came the next question : Why should anyone want to keep it ? And there was only one answer to that, too, and that was : Because it had a real value that none of us had understood. None of us, that is, except this one person. And then I couldn't help remembering that after all the metal plate had come out of that buried chamber, and that even if the site hadn't cast up anything good yet, it really *was* Mycenæan, and there was always that outside possibility that this might be a tomb, and might have something fine in it. I considered who had had the opportunity and the knowledge to substitute this new fake for our old one. I'd given the original to Bruce. He'd shown it to Dermot Crane and David Keyes, and then given it to Dermot to put in the safe overnight. And the next day David had carried it to Athens. That gave both of them opportunity. Both of them knew where it came from, both of them had specialist knowledge, and might very well have recognised this as a real find. And in that case either of them would have known enough to realise that we'd struck it rich, that the untapped chamber might be full of similar things.

" That was Dermot and David. Stavros had seen it, too, but he wasn't so likely to see anything remarkable in it. Nor were any of the workmen. I thought and thought, and always I came back to Dermot and David. The one could have made the substitution in the night. He kept the keys of the safe, and there were quite a few fragments of bronze and stuff among the rubble round Pirithoön, things of no special interest, that could have provided the material for the copy. The other could have changed them on the journey, or even in Athens, before he delivered the packet to Professor Barclay."

" But even supposing that your suspects did recognise a find, and realise the probability that there were many more pieces where it came from," I said, " faking up a copy wouldn't enable them to possess themselves of anything more than this one prize. The tomb—if it was a tomb— would still be opened. Bruce wouldn't have given up on account of one small setback."

Crispin turned his head and looked directly at me again, and his eyes were wide and dark. It was like looking down a long, long tunnel into the middle of his being, so far withdrawn that though all the gates lay open I couldn't distinguish anything of what passed within.

" No," he said, " Bruce wouldn't have given up for one setback. But that didn't matter any more, did it ? That had been taken care of, too. Bruce was dead. Nobody else believed in his passion for Pirithoön. Nobody else had the money, in any case, to carry on with the work. Once Bruce was dead, the dig was as good as closed. My mother would take me back to England. Dermot Crane would go back to Athens as soon as he'd tidied up the site and paid everybody off. David would go back to his job at London University. Pirithoön would lie there, just as it was, with the tomb still undisturbed, safe as houses until the one person who had plans for it came along at leisure to help himself. Either publicly, for the kudos of a tremendous find that should have gone to Bruce's credit, or privately, for the gold. Wasn't it convenient for that one person that the lintel of the citadel gateway fell on Bruce, and killed him ? In the night, when there weren't any witnesses ? "

CHAPTER VIII

So it was out, and now I understood part, at least, of the load he carried. It wasn't easy to grasp. The day was too sunny, the house too quiet, the garden too ordered and demure outside the open window. The idea of murder didn't go with this place. But I had only to turn my glance inwards to see the grey hill among the other grey hills, striated with reddish tints among the rocks, and the vast, Cyclopean fragments of the citadel walls, and the fallen block of stone, and Bruce's handsome head turning upward open eyes at the infinitely remote and brilliant sky of Greece. And beyond, the tumbled, turbulent landscape of the Argolid mountains, folded olive-grey valleys, smoky fig-trees, scarlet of anemones like blood across the hilltop, for it was in the spring.

" The police investigated at once," I heard myself saying, not wanting to believe what I saw. " You yourself seem to have been the first person on the scene after the stone fell. No one else questioned that the death was accidental. If you wanted to kill someone, would you in reason choose that method ? Even supposing it was possible ? "

" I might," said Crispin, in a thin, quiet voice, " supposing I'd already put a bullet or a knife in him first. Who's to know, after a man's had best part of a ton of stone dropped on him, how many injuries he had before it fell, and whether he was dead or alive ? "

" The ruins were known to be insecure," I argued, talking to myself as much as to him.

" Exactly," said Crispin, bitterly smiling. " Nobody was at all likely to question that it was accidental death. Nobody was even going to know of the circumstances that made it a little too opportune to be accidental—a little too opportune for someone. If I hadn't opened the parcel, nobody ever would have known. And as it is, nobody knows but us two."

" You've never spoken to anyone about this before ? "

" No, never to anyone."

I didn't ask him why, there was no need. Once the idea was admitted, there was no longer any possibility of broaching it to anyone, because the killer might have been anyone. The shadowy " he " stood behind every man in Pirithoön, and Crispin was alone. Utterly alone, sealed off from all speech, because no one could be trusted.

" If I'd been able to see Stavros alone," he said rather sadly, " I might have—— But I didn't. My mother kept me from going near all the business that went on on the site, with the police, and the local officials, and everything connected with my father's death. And Stavros was busy in the thick of it. I never had a chance to speak to him."

" And no chance to look at the place where the stone had fallen, either ? If someone really did dislodge it with a crowbar or something like that—and I suppose if it was precariously balanced already that would be possible—there might have been some signs to be found."

" I went there that night," said Crispin, " when everybody was in bed. I got out of the window, it was quite easy, our villa was mostly on one story. I had a torch, but I had to be careful how I used it. There wasn't any guard on the place. What would have been the good ? Nobody thought it anything but a tragic accident. The stonework by the gate was very much crumbled. The earth inside the walls had been built up in a ramp, you know, with a walk along the top, only it was badly broken up. So a man could easily walk up to the level of the lintel, and use a lever under it. How shaky it was before I don't know, though everybody said it was unsafe. But in all that crumbling stone it was impossible to say what marks were new and what were old, at least by night. In daylight maybe I could have done better. I only know that I felt absolutely sure it could have been done like that. My father already dead, and laid on the ground underneath the stone, and a crowbar levering under the rear corner—— It could hardly matter to a foot this way or that how accurately the stone fell."

He discussed this appalling possibility with the unblinking objectivity of a scientist, making accurate assessments and reasonable guesses where facts were missing. But there was nothing cold or detached about the passion with which he had concentrated his whole being into the pursuit of Bruce's murderer. I understood that now. Vaguely I saw the shadow of his purpose enormous behind him. I wondered how he endured its weight and its smothering darkness.

" What did you do then ? " I asked him, aware from the inward-looking fire of his eyes that there was something more, something fabulous, to tell about that night.

" I went into the tomb," said Crispin.

His voice was quiet, and his face very still. There was something of awe and astonishment in his very mildness, as if the monstrous power and significance of what he remembered had tamed and charmed him for a moment back into a child. He folded his hands in his lap, holding on to the humanity of his flesh, so that his own reality might not be blown away in the hurricane of time rushing backwards.

" Someone had been there already and moved two of the pieces of the stone so that our entrance was covered. But I managed to move them, they weren't too heavy. I'd brought a rope from the huts on the dig, and I tied it round one of the stones that was massive enough to hold my weight, and squeezed through the crevice, and let myself down the drifted rubble inside until I came to the stone-paved floor of the vestibule. It was just like Nikos had described it there, partly silted up with fallen stones and earth, but the entrance wasn't blocked. I had only to pick my way over the piles of fallen stuff, and go in. The doorway was so tall I could only shine my torch on part of it at a time, and inside it was darker than anything you can imagine, and the air was something more than air, heavy, smelling of earth and thick spices, but mostly of earth. It wasn't unpleasant. Only terrible. You know what I mean——"

I said : " I know ! "

" There were five people in the tomb. They were lying on raised slabs of stone, hollowed out a little on top to hold the bodies. There was nothing else, except a few pots and things, and the shape of the walls going up into the dark and drawing in gradually, course by course, overhead. There was one place where a few stones had fallen, I think perhaps in some earth tremor very long ago, and part of the wall had sagged inward and rolled over one of the skeletons, and broken it to pieces. When I stepped through the doorway I nearly stepped on some of the bones. The skull was there, by my feet, and an arm bone, still lying in three or four metal bracelets. The other four bodies were lying in their places, untouched."

His voice was level and slow, as though he spoke out of the remote distance of hypnosis, seeing again the immemorial hidden place, and smelling the heavy, cool, earthen darkness. He was not afraid ; he had not been afraid then. Or if he had, it was the kind of quivering, eager fear Ulysses felt when he pressed unnecessarily and impiously forward into perilous places, driven by the divine, new, heretical curiosity which was the Greek gift to the world. It had been too wonderful for fear to have any effect on him.

" They had on the remnants of robes, bits of fabrics still ornamented with patterns, only so dim I couldn't detect colours. I think two of them were women. Two of the

intact ones were not much more than skeletons, the other
two still had flesh, dried and mummified. All of them were
covered with ornaments. They had breastplates and armlets
and collars of gold, the women had gold necklaces, and all
of them had frontlets of gold, covering their foreheads,
with a tongue curved down over the bridge of the nose, and
wings folded down over the temples and cheeks. Not just
thin gold leaf applied to the faces, but masks of gold like
symbolical helms. And that was what Nikos had brought
up out of the doorway, that night when we first broke in
there. It was the gold mask that had rolled away with the
skull, when the fall of earth shattered the one body. As old
as Troy, maybe older ! Think of it ! And we'd had it in
our hands, and hadn't known what it was. We'd worked
it off on Bruce as a silly joke, and all the time it was the
justification for the whole of his life, if only we'd realised it.
I don't mean a scholarly justification—but a spiritual one,
somehow."

"They were still that," I said, "those relics down there.
You had only to go to Dermot—or to the police, since
you felt you couldn't be sure of Dermot—and tell them
what you'd found, and the tomb would have been opened
at once. There you had Bruce's memorial in your hands.
He would have been Almond of Pirithoön as long as research
lasted. And you could have served yet another purpose at
the same time. You had only to speak, and the tomb would
have become a national and international wonder, if it
lives up to the promise you saw in it. And whoever benefited
by it, your father's murderer wouldn't. You could have
prevented him from touching the hoard he killed for, and
made your father's name, all in one stroke, at the expense
of a few words. And you never said a word ! "

"No," said Crispin, "I never said a word. Never until
now."

"But for God's sake, why not ? "

He turned his head and gave me a long, dark, self-contained look, and I thought for a moment that I had somehow disappointed him, and he wasn't going to answer. But he had begun this unburdening—easy or hard, it was certainly that—on my account, not on his own, and he held in reserve only those inmost and most personal parts of his experience which could not be shared without violating something essential in himself. After a moment he said : " It's quite true, I could have prevented him from getting his hands on either the gold or the glory, if I'd gone to the police. But I still shouldn't have known who he was. And neither would they. Never ! They'd already inquired into Bruce's death, and concluded it was a tragic accident. Dermot claimed to have left him safe and well in the office at about eleven o'clock, and come to bed. Nobody else had seen him since David went off to the village inn, where he lived, at ten, just about the time I'd said good night to him and gone to bed myself. No, there'd never have been anything to show who came back so late, who got him to go up to the Acropolis, who killed him there, and tipped the stone over on the top of him. Nobody would ever have believed it was anything but an accident. There wasn't any evidence. And there was only one way I could see of getting any. I had to find out who killed my father. His memorial could wait for that. He'd get it just the same in the end."

" So what did you do ? " I asked, though I was already half-way to knowing the answer.

" I took all the golden ornaments and hid them in my clothes, the bracelets and armlets and necklaces in my pockets and on my arms, the pectorals and face masks buttoned inside my shirt and jacket. I stripped even the skeleton that was broken, and I put the bones all together in the moulded slab of stone. I didn't like disturbing them, I did it as gently as I could. But if being dead is just the end of it," said Crispin simply, "it didn't do them any wrong. And if it isn't, and they knew what was happening, then they'd know the motives, too. And I think they wouldn't grudge me the use of their property."

I was beginning to feel the same way, but it sent a chill down my spine to hear him say it, and with such unassuming authority.

" Are you trying to tell me," I said, " that you brought all that gold away with you, and never said a word to anybody else about it ? "

" Yes. What else could I do ? I brought it out of the tomb with me, and put back the stones just as I'd found them. I hid the gold in my suitcases—they were already packed ready to leave next day—and went back to bed. And next day my mother and I left for Athens, and about four days later we flew home."

" But how on earth did you get them through the Customs ? And without even your mother knowing anything about it ? "

" It wasn't difficult. Only uncomfortable ! Of course, if we hadn't been the survivors of a tragedy the regulations might have been more stringently applied. Or if I'd been a few years older. I know that. I had to take advantage of things like that, or I couldn't have done it. And then, you know, thin gold plates aren't all that bulky. I had them all on me—nothing in my cases but my clothes and things. I had all the bracelets and armlets right up both arms from elbow to shoulder, strapped in position with adhesive plaster so that they wouldn't move and clash together, and all the breast-plates and masks strapped to my body under my shirt in the same way, and the necklaces round my neck. From shoulders to hips I was stiff with gold. It felt like being in plaster from an accident—broken ribs, or something—and it made me look thicker-set than I am, and my clothes were rather tight. But then, no one who knew me well enough to notice the difference was going to see me on

the journey. The worst spot was the English Customs—
I mean the one I was most afraid of—but it went off without
a hitch. I was only a kid of fifteen, why should they suppose
I should be hiding anything ? "

" And you understood, of course," I said, " that you
must have been breaking I don't know how many laws in
the process ? "

" Yes, naturally, but there was nothing else I could do."

" And you also understood—to come down to more
homely terms—that you were stealing from the Greek
Government ? "

" Yes, I knew that, and I was sorry. But I don't mean to
keep the things, they'll all go back to the Greek Government in the end. I had to have them for a time, that's all.
The man who killed my father to get them would only wait
until everybody was off the scene to go back and plunder
the tomb. And when he found himself forestalled, and the
gold gone, he would have to follow it. Nobody's going to
write off a treasure like that as a dead loss, after he's killed
for it. It was the only way I could think of to find out for
certain, the only way of inducing him to betray himself. So
I had to have the gold with me. And wherever I went, it
had to stay with me. I knew that if I had it, sooner or later
he'd come for it."

" And that's why you made all the schools too hot to
hold you," I said thoughtfully. " Because the stuff was
here, and this was the chosen ground on which you'd
elected to encounter Bruce's murderer."

" It's Bruce's house," said Crispin. " I should have
hated that school, anyhow, I expect. But even if I'd liked
it, I couldn't have stayed there."

" It seems to me a rather chancy assumption," I said
carefully. " that he's bound to turn up here looking for his
plunder. Even supposing, for the sake of argument, that
he doesn't, as you say, give up so easily, but sets out to

look for it. He may very well conclude that the tomb has been rifled since Bruce's death, since the original mask was found only a few days before; and therefore that it has been rifled by someone belonging to the dig. He may even consider following up and investigating each one in turn, in search of it. But—if you'll forgive the implications— how long is it going to be before he gets round to you? Not before he's cancelled out all your elders. He may even suspect that some local person has happened on the broken stone quite by chance since the dig was closed, and lifted the contents. He may never consider you as a possibility at all."

"I've taken care of that," said Crispin, rearing his head again with that haughty awareness with which he habitually put on the man, and thrust the boy away from him as an expense he could not afford. "I couldn't leave anything to chance. No, he won't have wasted time on anyone else, or on looking round the local people, and he won't write me off as negligible. Because I left him a message inside the tomb. I left one of Bruce's visiting cards, with this address on it, on the edge of the stone slab where the skeletons lay, and I signed my name on the back of it. So I knew he must come," said Crispin, looking at me straight and steadily across the room, "and, you see, he has come."

CHAPTER IX

Down in the sunlit garden, among the roses, Dorothy was walking between Dermot Crane and David Keyes. I watched them stop to admire a coral-flame bush of Fashion, and then pass onward slowly, and out of sight round a corner of the greenhouse.

I looked back over Crispin's story, and tried to see all the events with an unprejudiced eye, but always I was left with two stony facts which would not be explained away. Firstly, I no longer doubted Crispin's flat statement that an exchange of masks had been effected, somewhere between the package leaving Bruce's hands and reaching Professor Barclay's. And secondly, Crispin's desk had undoubtedly been broken into by someone, looking for something. What could it be but the gold ? I couldn't get round these two things, no matter how arduously I reasoned. I even began to reason aloud, as though a conviction like his was vulnerable to argument.

" If only Crane had come, then, or only Keyes, you'd have taken that as proof positive that he was the guilty one ? And yet what could possibly be more natural than that Crane should come to visit you and your mother as soon as he returned to England ? He even had business to clear up for your mother in Greece, your father's outstanding bills to pay, and so on. Of course he would come to report, and to see that you were all right. And Keyes, too, though he had less official connection with your mother, might very well take the opportunity to pay a courtesy call when he happened to be in the neighbourhood. I know the business of the mask can't be explained away. I know some of the other circumstances are highly suspicious, given your special knowledge. But you mustn't make too much of the appearance here of these two men, because to any unprejudiced observer it's obvious that nothing could be more natural. And their turning up the same day makes it seem more innocent, not less. Unless you think they're in collusion ? "

" No," said Crispin definitely. " Only one man was involved in my father's murder. I've been over all that ground, you know, time after time. But there's no need to argue about it, in any case. If I'm right, and he's come to the decoy—whichever of them *he* may be—then all we have to do is wait for him to make the next move. He wants the gold, he'll have to set about finding it. And if he's innocent, and here in all innocence, then he won't know anything about the gold—will he ?—so he'll just stay over the week-end and go peacefully away. But I don't believe that, and you don't, either. I don't have to prove that one of these two knew about the gold, and knew that I had it— he's already proved that for us." He cast a significant glance at the desk. " I don't even have to prove which one it is— he's going to prove that, too, before the week-end is over. All I have to do is wait."

" And I—what have I to do ? " And indeed, I wondered, in the face of his certainty, what there was for anyone to do, for it seemed that if he was right the train of events had already been fired long ago, and nobody could extricate Crispin from his own trap. He had taken good care that nobody should have the chance.

" As far as I'm concerned," he said with emphasis, " nothing. I've never asked you for anything. I haven't told you this now so that you could help me, but only so that if you insist on gate-crashing the affair you will at least know what you're up against." He caught the note of severity in his own voice, and unexpectedly blushed. " I'm sorry, I don't mean to be rude, or ungrateful, either. It isn't that I don't trust you, and—and like you. I think you'd be fine to have by me in a scrap. But this is different. It's my responsibility. I didn't want anyone else involved in it. I wanted the stage cleared of everybody but me and my enemy. But since you wouldn't go, I had to let you understand that this is serious. It's already a life and death matter, why should he stick at killing again ? But now you know, and there's nothing more I can do."

He got up from the bed, and went and helped himself to a cigarette from the box on the desk. His hand was trembling a little, but I think from embarrassment only, and a slight fear that he had said too much, and failed to say it as well as he would have liked. He set himself hard standards.

" There's a great deal more you can do, if you choose," I said. " You can tell me, for instance, what's supposed to happen when the hypothetical ' he ' does reveal himself by coming dunning you for the information nobody else can give him. Are the police, do you suppose, going to be convinced on this evidence that a crime was ever committed ? Let alone that because ' he ' is a thief he must therefore also be a murderer. You said yourself, if you remember, that nobody would ever believe Bruce's death was anything but an accident. Are the police in England going to take less convincing than the police in the Peloponnese ? "

He looked up at me, over the still-burning match, with a face of momentary blank incomprehension, and repeated : " Police ? " as though I'd used a foreign word he'd never heard before. Then the match burned his fingers, and he swore abstractedly, and shook it out, staring at me all the while with a face still blank, but no longer empty of understanding. His shoulders lifted a little. He smiled. But he didn't make any reply. I couldn't, however, have had a plainer answer, or a more frightening one.

So the police had no part in this ! He felt no need of them. They had never for one moment entered into his calculations. What had to be done, Crispin proposed to do himself. He'd told the simple truth when he said that there was room on the stage for only two characters, himself and his enemy.

In the worst moment of revelation I'd ever had, I recognised to whom I was talking. Not for nothing had he learned Greek almost as he learned English, and imbibed Oedipus Rex and the Oresteia almost before he was done with his mother's milk. Already I'd felt a queer stab of knowledge and foreboding when he put on the man, and uttered that strangely ritualistic " my father " where the boy would have said Bruce. This was no longer merely Crispin Almond, it was Orestes himself, taking upon him the inescapable filial burden, planning vengeance for his father, dragging down upon himself such Furies as English law has left us, and believe me, they can be Furies enough. I understood, marvelling how like an ordinary human boy he looked as he made a second attempt at lighting his cigarette, why he had said so coldly that for him there was no point in studying. The course and the duration of his life were already prescribed and accepted. He didn't expect to survive. And if he survived, he was assured it would be in lifelong segregation from a society which did not subscribe to his classic conceptions of a son's duty. He was absolutely dedicated. He had written himself off.

I was in full view of my own image in the mirror as this appalling knowledge sank its knife into me ; and neither of us turned a hair. Even the refinements of what I knew couldn't yet register properly. For instance, I began in a rush : " But what I don't understand is why you didn't ——" and then bit off : "——tell your mother ! " Just in time ; because it needed only that prod to make it perfectly plain why he hadn't told Dorothy. Orestes had a mother, too. It was she who had the axe in her hand when Agamemnon was murdered.

But it was crazy! Dorothy hadn't even been there! She'd arrived the following day from Athens——

From Athens! I felt the second knife, all right, it had me up off the end of the bed and across the room like a convulsion of angina, trying to get out of range of the shock and the pain, but it was everywhere. Athens! What a fool I must have been to miss the significance of that, and after hearing it twice, once from Keyes, once from Crispin. What was Dorothy doing in Athens? A concert tour? I'd followed her notices, but I'd never heard of her playing in Athens. And even if she was there on such innocuous business, *how did she get to Pirithoön in the time*? Bruce's body was found shortly after midnight. Dorothy arrived from Athens half-way through the following afternoon. She'd read about the tragedy in the newspapers? Impossible! She must have left Athens by mid-morning at the very latest, and the morning papers couldn't possibly have carried the news even as a stop-press item. . The authorities discovered she was in Athens, and conveyed the news to her? But she didn't use the name Almond in her professional career, she played as Dorothy Grieve. And in any case there wouldn't have been time for them to trace her hotel and get in touch with her so quickly. No, Dorothy knew because someone at the dig wired or telephoned her the news—because, therefore, someone at the dig knew exactly where to find her.

If I could work that out, I thought, so could he. He'd gone over that certainty in his own mind time after time, and no one knew better than he that someone at Pirithoön must have been in constant communication with Dorothy in Athens. And no one could more readily jump to the conclusion that the " he " who contacted Dorothy and told her to come and fetch her son was the same " he " who had stolen the mask and killed Bruce. There'd been clues enough, heaven knows ! That terrible thing he'd once said to her, and then hated himself for saying, but never taken back again—that ought to have been enough for me. " Don't practise on me ! If you want to be in form for Dermot——"

Yes, Dermot was the one on whom Crispin had staked his soul. David's arrival had been a setback to his certainty, but it was still Dermot he had cast for Dorothy's lover. What was he likely to be to her but a lover, that secret correspondent in Bruce's camp, who wired her to come and get the boy off the scene as soon as the murder was committed ? Apart from the sudden revelation of the gold mask, which made this the inspired moment to time the murder and take the treasure too, Dorothy and a lover would have another, a long-standing motive for getting rid of Bruce Almond, who didn't believe in divorce, and considered his wife bound to him for ever. If that was how Crispin had reasoned—and his whole attitude to his mother bore it out, now that I had the clue—then he must be assuming that the pair had had murder in mind for some time, and the gold mask had been only the additional incentive which had caused the lover to act at that particular moment. That done, her part had been to rush in and play the solicitous mother, and remove the too adult, too intelligent son from the scene, so that the dig and the death and the gold together could be buried in forgetfulness. And Dermot's—since he was cast in that part in Crispin's mind—had been to stay behind and arrange the burial, and then quietly, discreetly, take possession of the gold, before coming home to pay court to the widow, and make a respectable match with her.

Yes, in Crispin's eyes Dorothy was implicated in Bruce's death to the hilt. They had both had a double motive. Perhaps the man came first with her, the gold with him, when the golden inducement was added to the other. But each of them stood to gain the lover and the gold, too. Motive enough for half a dozen murders.

And what, then, I could hardly bear to wonder, had Crispin in mind for Dorothy ?

" Perhaps we ought to go down," said Crispin, " before they begin to wonder what we're up to."

That was all he said. And how can you argue against accusations that have never been made, reconstructions which have never been stated ? I knew now what was going on in his mind as well as if he'd expressed it, but he hadn't expressed it, and I couldn't take him by the shoulders, and shake him, and say : " Look here, that may all be perfectly logical reasoning, but it's also perfect nonsense. If you knew your mother as well as I know her, you'd know that she could never plot, or over-value the kind of respectability divorce preserves, or hurt a hair of Bruce's head." And in any case, even if he'd said just one word that would have let me bring the rest into daylight, what would have been the use ? He didn't know Dorothy at all, he was merely her son, and that didn't help him to know the first thing about her.

So it seemed to me that it was up to me. If there was no part in it for the police, all the more urgent became the part that had been accidentally written in for me. I did know Dorothy, I was far enough in Crispin's confidence now to understand that someone had to take action quickly, in order to forestall the inevitable development of the drama he had planned. All he had to do, he had said, was to wait until " he " made the next move. But what I had to do was to move first. For Dorothy's sake, but for Crispin's sake too. By that time I didn't know which of them mattered more to me. I did know that between them they made up a world.

So I simply said : " Yes, perhaps we ought. Don't

forget your camera. If you prefer, we can reappear separately."

But on the way downstairs I did ask him outright, the only way it could be asked, so that he could give me a straight answer or tell me it was none of my business: " Where is the gold now ? "

He looked up at me and smiled a little, rather engagingly, and then very firmly closed his lips, and made no answer at all. And I didn't press him. But I did issue a warning of my own, almost worthy of him at his most punctilious.

" Mind," I said, " I've made no promises about what I intend to do. You can take it that your confidences are respected, of course, which means I can't bring in the police or anyone else. But you did confide in me, remember. for my protection, maybe, but I didn't ask you to protect me, the choice was yours. I'm debarred from passing on anything you've said to anyone else, but I'm not debarred from taking action on it myself. In any way which occurs to me as possible and useful. Agreed ? "

Rather grudgingly, rather anxiously, he said that he supposed that was fair enough. But he wished I wouldn't.

" No holds barred ? " I said.

Reluctantly, but smiling too, he said : " No holds barred ! "

CHAPTER X

I THOUGHT the whole thing over, and could think of only two courses of action which might help us. The first and most obvious—and hopeless—was to run to earth the one real piece of evidence, the original gold frontlet Nikos had brought out of the tomb. If one thing was reasonably certain in the whole nightmare, it was that whoever had extracted that from its parcel and substituted another for it still had the original in his possession. To locate that would be to identify our opponent, which was the biggest step towards being able to deal with him. On the other hand, it seemed to me very unlikely that either Crane or Keyes would travel with the thing in his suitcase. However, there was no point in leaving the search unmade just because it was not particularly likely to yield results.

After dinner it wasn't difficult to get an hour to myself on the pretext of writing letters. Keyes, as it turned out, played the piano rather well, and had persuaded Dorothy to get out her violin, and they were trying over the Beethoven C Minor sonata. Crane wasn't likely to leave the room while Dorothy played. Crispin certainly wouldn't leave his observation post again while these three remained together. I had them all off my hands for a while, and off my heels, too.

Crane's possessions were arranged meticulously on his tallboy and in the drawers. Like Orlando, he was somewhat point-device in his accoutrements. Everything he had with him seemed to be open to view, except the brief-case which lay on his bed, and that was locked. I should probably have had qualms about opening it, if he—or someone else—hadn't already opened Crispin's desk; as it was, I flatter myself I made the neater job of the two, with the aid of a small nail-file, and a safety-pin. It was a long time, a very long time, since I'd done anything of the kind, but either I hadn't lost the knack, or else this was a peculiarly childish lock. But there was nothing at all incriminating inside. A couple of road maps, a detective novel, a sheaf of papers which appeared to be the draft of an article on some Crusader castle missed by the young Lawrence. He was obviously a man who re-wrote time after time, and swopped adjective for adjective with a perfectionist fervour. Which was more or less what I should have expected of him, on what little I'd seen of him. There was also a folded specialist journal, a small wallet of photographs of details in some unidentifiable frieze, and a letter without an envelope, Dorothy's few scrawled lines inviting him warmly to come and stay at the Lawns as long as he liked.

She was no letter writer, and abbreviated to such an extent that she had almost invented a new system of shorthand. Nothing in this note she might not have written to an old and casual acquaintance—me, for instance—in the same circumstances. " Dear D——" How typical of her hasty missives that they were always directed to initials, not names. I hadn't seen the impetuous hand for years, but I could never mistake it or forget it.

I put everything back in its place, and coaxed the lock to close on the innocuous contents of the brief-case. And that was that ; a blank, but no more nor less than I'd expected.

David's room was no more productive than Crane's, but at least it made a change. His stuff was all casual, very casually kept, and scattered about the bed and the room as though a hurricane had blown through the place, or a large and playful dog. His reading matter was a motoring magazine and a couple of assorted travel Penguins. He hadn't any gold, either.

I'd finished with them both, and the C Minor was still sounding distantly from the garden-room. I was passing Crispin's door when something made me turn sharply, and slip into the room instead. Perhaps searching rooms had become a habit by then; or perhaps the thought that clarified a few seconds later had already established itself firmly enough in my mind to start issuing orders. As I closed the door very softly and carefully behind me, and looked round the empty room, I knew what I was looking for, and it wasn't gold. Not here. He'd told me flatly that it wasn't here to be found, in any case.

Crispin had supplied a wealth of evidence to establish his attitude to his mother, in spite of a self-control very few men, let alone boys, could have equalled. But on consideration, not quite so much evidence to account for it. To have cast his mother as Clytemnestra, as he'd done, he must surely have had some more solid ground for suspicion, something more suggestive altogether than merely her too prompt arrival at Pirithoön. Something equally capable of an innocent explanation, that went without saying; but compromising enough to establish at once a case to be answered, a case which needed an answer. If he was holding something which tended to incriminate Dorothy, then I had to know what it was. How else could I refute its evidence?

All the same, I hesitated to touch anything of his. The confidences he'd bestowed on me might be of his own choice, and carry always a singular reserve about them, but they were still confidences. All the same, this was no time to stand on punctilio. Crispin was playing—no, that was unjust, nothing in the world had ever been further removed from play—Crispin was arrogating to himself, for reasons sufficiently tragic and terrible, the right to dispose of three lives, one of them his own. And in a way he was justified— not by the law, true, but by the law shall no man living be justified !—but he was also wrong. Wrong about Dorothy, wrong about himself. Anybody who was heart and soul on his side had got to play this hand not only against the unidentified enemy, but against Crispin, too. He had accepted that the completion of his vengeance would be the end of his life, whether he survived it or not. But I didn't accept it. As far as I was concerned, Crispin was not expendable—not even by Crispin.

The fact that he'd left his keys on the desk gave me an additional twinge. He hadn't envisaged this when he agreed grudgingly that I had the right to act on what I knew. Still, there was no help for it. I unlocked the desk, and went carefully through the array of letters, pictures, old press-cuttings and articles from learned journals, which Crispin had salvaged from his father's past. Nothing there seemed to touch on Dorothy. The drawers of the desk cast up a touching collection of materials wonderfully inappropriate to Crispin as I knew him, but recalling painfully what he ought to have been. All the equipment of innocence was there, the half-assembled models, light balsa-wood and thin alloys for aircraft, two or three miniature racing cars, a wealth of photographic material, chemicals, printing frames, enlarger, sheaves of experimental prints, little jewel-coloured pots of paints. School apparatus, too, atlases, geometrical instruments, cases of pencils all carefully sharpened, a few sketches, enthusiastic, rapid and forceful, with a lot of Dorothy in them, though Dorothy couldn't draw a line. I'd never seen him touch any of these things, most of them I didn't even know he possessed. He'd turned his back on childish things, not because he despised them, not even because he'd lost his taste for them ; it was just that he was aware that they were not for him.

But that, I thought, all the same, is the kind of boy he was meant to be, a perfectly normal young creature explod-ing in half a dozen hobbies in turn, and dropping them as he

outgrew them and grabbed at something bigger. And the
thought made me feel justified, and the rest of my search
was shameless. But it was also fruitless.

I'd been through everything but his bookshelves, which
filled one whole alcove in the room ; and they were going
to take far too long. Those two downstairs couldn't go on
playing Beethoven for ever. All the same, I went over to
the shelves and examined them rapidly. In the lowest
shelves, which were deeper than the rest, were all his earliest
books, the lavish picture-books from babyhood, the first
inevitable infant classics, worn with love and use, with
stubbed corners and frayed edges. Then the boyish books,
usual and unusual, school stories, Indians, travel, adventure,
a lot of maps, understandably a great deal of archæology,
fine books of photographs from Egypt and the Middle East,
Bruce's gifts, no doubt. They hadn't lived very much in
this house, only for a few months now and then, between
journeys, but it had always been their base, and it was here
that Crispin had deposited his treasures, all the accumulation
of his expanding life. The Greek language made its entrance
early, and side by side with the originals he kept the English
translations. I ran my finger along the titles, and it stopped
of its own volition on the Oresteia, those three volumes of
Aeschylus with more blood, violence and grandeur in them
than in all the campaigns that ever were fought.

If only I'd used my wits, I needn't have made that long
search, I thought, feeling the shiver of prophetic cold
stroking my spine. If he has anything to hide, anything
that can be slipped in a book, for instance, I ought to have
had sense enough to know which book he'd choose.

It was the second volume I took out, the Choephori, the
Libation-Bearers. It fell open of itself when I opened my
hand, and left me staring at the last dialogue between
Orestes and his mother.

Orestes : I mean to kill you close beside him. While
he lived You preferred him to my father. Sleep with him
in death ; For you love him, and hate the man you should
have loved.

Clytemnestra : I gave you your life : let me then live
out my own.

Orestes : Live ? Here, in my house—you, my father's
murderer ?

So now I knew what Crispin had in mind for Dorothy.
Not whether he had the ferocity to go through with it,
when it came to the point, but what he felt it to be incum-
bent upon him to do. And in case I'd missed the point, a
folded slip of paper slid down the open page into my palm.
I unfolded it with the certainty that it could be neither
accidental nor irrelevant.

It was a piece torn from the top half of a sheet of note-
paper, and folded across twice, carelessly enough, as though
to slip into a book to keep somebody's place. Which was
patently not its purpose in this book. The address embossed
in the right-hand corner was that of a hotel, in Kolonaki,
in Athens, and handwriting and sense began like an echo,
like an optical illusion : " Dear D——"

Even supposing I could have forgotten, in all those years,
Dorothy's dashing hand, that letter of invitation to Dermot
Crane rose before my eyes and swam into alignment with
this.

" Dear D.,
  " So happy to get your letter. It makes all the difference
in the world to me to know that you're there in P. Only
do be careful he doesn't get to know I'm in Greece, and
you're writing me re——"

There it broke off, torn through in the middle of a word.

What word, I wondered? Regularly? It was what sprang to mind. And even so, there was nothing in the text that couldn't be explained in a hundred innocent ways, if only I could think of them, or make them sound convincing when I had thought of them. But all I could do was imagine Crispin picking up this fragment of his mother's writing, somewhere " there in P.," and looking from Dermot Crane to David Keyes, trying to discover the mind's complexion in the face, and divine which of them had been writing to Athens letters which made the recipient " so happy," and which of them it was that had orders to " be careful he doesn't get to know I'm in Greece." Dear Dermot? Dear David? She was always in such a hurry with letters, what a pity she had no time to write names in full. David, I remembered, had asked to come and join Bruce's party only about four weeks before the disaster, which was suggestive up to a point. On the other hand, Dermot was older, more likely to be in Dorothy's confidence, even, I had to admit, more likely to be attractive to her——

That was when I realised that I was reasoning as if I believed her guilty. *Dorothy!* And I thought, pushing away the suspicions with which he'd infected me, damn Crispin! and then took it back as frantically, because, poor little devil, somebody *had* damned him, only too surely, unless I found out how to work a miracle. He must be wrong about Dorothy, in spite of a dozen incriminating letters, he might be wrong about other things, but he wasn't wrong about the gold mask that vanished and the copy left in its place, and I was beginning to be certain that he wasn't wrong about Bruce's death, either. Somebody had planned his murder, somebody had executed the plan. Only not Dorothy! It couldn't be Dorothy!

And I thought, as I put the slip of paper back into its place, and the book back on the shelf, I'll bet that's what somebody was fool enough to say about Clytemnestra, too.

Not the queen ! It couldn't be the queen ! She can't have known anything about it !

I was astonished to find that my forehead was running with sweat, as though the room were burning hot. I went and leaned out from the open window into the freshness of the late evening, and the scent of the roses came up like a wave of delight, and the music with it, offered and withdrawn upon a changeable breeze. The end of the last movement. Keyes played really well, but they were both brittle with some tension that must have been in the air about the boy. How did it help anybody, that I should suddenly know beyond question and beyond hope that I was still in love with Dorothy, always had been, always would be, as long as I lived ?

I looked round the room quickly, to make sure everything was back in its place, and then I went to the bathroom and bathed my face in cold water. By the time they'd finished criticising their own performance of the Beethoven, he accusing himself and extolling her, she somewhat ironically declining his bouquets, I was just coming in from the garden, as though I'd been out for a breath of air before bedtime.

Dermot was in a wing-chair close to the open window. Crispin was sitting on a hassock with his arms round his knees. His eyes, light blue in calm, proceeded—wandered was too purposeless a word—from face to face, missing nothing, no movement of an eyelid, no tightening of a muscle in a cheek, nothing that could enlarge his knowledge of his potential enemies.

And I was among them. I saw that when the eyes in their shining, withdrawn intelligence rested upon me. They did not change. Without hate, even with understanding, he measured in me the makings of one more enemy. And this time I understood why he could never give his complete confidence to any man, never place reliance in any

man's will to help him, so long as he distrusted Dorothy.
I knew now why he had once said to me that I might be
useful, if I were on his side. " But you wouldn't be."

To him all men were potential allies, not for him, but for
Dorothy. Not one of them could be trusted to take sides
against her. Never. Not even with the truth.

And now I didn't even know if he was right about me.
I only knew that there was nobody but me to get us all out
of this unbearable deadlock before the catastrophe over-
whelmed us all, and that if it wasn't attempted before this
week-end was over, it would, in any case, be too late.

CHAPTER XI

I SAT IN MY open window smoking until all the house was
quiet and dark. I'd used up all the possibilities of my first
course of action already without result, I was reduced to
the second. And this one had to get results, because it was
the only one I had left.

If Crispin's " he " was really here—let him be Dermot,
or David, or whoever he would—then the crisis was
inevitably upon us, and nothing could be done to avert it.
But what I might be able to do was to precipitate it, and
precipitate it somewhere away from the house, away from
Crispin, away from Dorothy. Crispin sat at the heart of the
cyclone, waiting with certainty for the enemy to come to
him ; but he could be certain only because he had the gold,
and was the only person in the world who could tell where
it was ; and his premise held good only so long as he and
the gold stayed together or, more accurately, as long as the
enemy believed that they were together. Should they be
separated, it was the gold " he " would follow.

Nobody knew better than I did that Crispin was never

likely to surrender his treasure into my keeping. But how, after all, could the enemy know that ? From the outside it might appear very probable indeed that a sixteen-year-old boy should find himself badly scared when it came to the point, and be only too glad to hand over his dangerous charge to some older person for safe-keeping. Supposing, for instance, that I were observed stealing away from Crispin's room by night, and then from the house, with something bulky and suggestive nursed tenderly under my arm ? The hunter must be watching the boy's every move, and every trail that started from him would demand investigation, especially a stealthy nocturnal trail, laid when all the house was asleep, and honest people, with no secrets to keep, were scarcely likely to be on the move. And supposing that he should swallow the bait, and follow me to some safe and secret place where he could observe at leisure my dispositions for the concealment of that queer something I'd brought away from the house with me ?

Yes, there might be something there. If he precipitated the showdown—well, I should at least be prepared for him. If he did not, if he hung back and waited for me to go away, satisfied that I'd been unobserved, and leave him to disinter the treasure in his own time—well, so much the better, the initiative would then be with me, and I could pull out the pin from the impending eruption at the best moment for my own plans.

And what would it prove ? That he was a thief ? Possibly. That he was a murderer ?

Not Bruce's, I concluded regretfully, that was past proving in this country, short of a confession, and it was very improbable that it could ever be proved even with a great deal of detective work in Greece.

My murderer——?

Well, that was also a possibility, as Crispin had punctiliously pointed out.

I am not a hero. I found that out during the war—most of us did, sooner or later—and I've had cause to confirm the observation several times since. Now that I'd run my nose into the cold, discouraging conviction that I might be planning the circumstances of my own demise, the old, queasy chill took me in the pit of the stomach, and plumped me down on the bed to reconsider what I was doing.

No fooling, Evelyn, this has stopped being a game. If the man who killed Bruce has followed Crispin here in pursuit of his gold, he'll kill for it again if need be. And what you're proposing to provide for him is a fine and private place in which to do it, and yourself as the victim if he proves an apter man of his hands than you. Just two people at the rendezvous. No part for the police, because there's nothing to offer them they would recognise as evidence, and also because the one thing in the whole involved business which they would acknowledge without hesitation as a crime happens to be Crispin's theft. Also, when it comes to the point, because you've given Crispin your word not to betray his confidences.

What, was I going to stick my neck out like this simply because I'd made a promise to Crispin ? I sat clutching my head and cursing myself for a lunatic, but I knew I was going to do just that.

And for God's sake, what did I hope to do, even if the decoy worked, even if I could spring my trap at the very moment when the murderer retrieved my lure, and catch him red-handed ? Then what ? Kill him ? How much was there to choose between that and being killed by him ? But yes, kill him if I had to. Bring him back alive if I could, and risk whether we could ever prove anything against him. At least then he would be identified, and Crispin's loot could be handed back voluntarily to the Greek Government. The best of a bad business. *If* it worked my way ! And if it didn't——

And all the time I knew that what really mattered was that it would be over, one way or the other, before Dorothy or Crispin need know anything about it. Whoever might be destroyed, they would be safe. And after all, I'd had some experience of intimate personal warfare, and could hold my own with most men ; and I should not be taken by surprise. Which of us would come out of it intact we should see. But Dorothy and Crispin would be safe.

After all, there'd never really been any question of what I must do, I knew that. She'd never stopped being the most important person in the world to me, and there was nothing I could do about it, and no longer any point in denying it. And the boy was inextricably part of her, whatever lamentable mischance had estranged them. I might as well admit, while I was about this testamentary stock-taking, that what caused me the sharpest pain when I saw them together was that he wasn't mine. But that needn't discourage me from taking the liberty of dying for him.

Not that I had the least intention of dying, of course, if I could help it. And I should be choosing the ground.

It had to be somewhere entirely plausible as a hiding-place, or he would suspect a trap. And it had to be somewhere with hazards that I knew far better than he could possibly know them, so that I could take advantage of the layout, and he could not. Like, for instance——?

The day had been long, and seemed longer, and my mind was blank for a while. It couldn't be anywhere too near the house, I couldn't risk it. It had to be somewhere screened from all interference. My own proceedings were not necessarily going to be any more legal than my enemy's. No, there had to be just two people present at that show-down, each one as isolated as the champions of chivalry who went out after dragons.

There was, of course, an obvious place, though it took me ten minutes to think of it. Our cave up there in the limestone hillside answered all the requirements. It was somewhere I knew at any rate reasonably well, and the chances were it would be quite unknown to the enemy. It afforded me room to manœuvre, and a showdown there was liable to be so private that it could go on to the death without being interrupted. And of all the feasible hiding-places between us and Wells, it was the most convincing.

So much for the place. As for the time, I discarded the idea of putting the plan into practice to-night. It was too late, the ground was not prepared yet. To-morrow night— if the enemy waited so long. And I could and would ward off any action until then by sticking to Crispin closer than a brother. No murderer, however bold and desperate, was going to walk up to the boy and demand his gold while a hefty tutor had him by the elbow.

Moreover, up to now we had instinctively avoided the appearance of being intimately in league, because that had suited Crispin's plans, and Crispin had been calling the tune. But now I had plans of my own, and they demanded rather that we should be seen to be hand in glove. Give me just one day of clinging like a shadow to his side, and looming up defensively to ward off all solitary approaches to him, and I should quite certainly be under suspicion by evening, and under intent observation when I crept out of the house at one o'clock in the morning with a bulky and misshapen brief-case under my arm. I needed to-morrow to set my scene.

At that moment it occurred to me that between now and to-morrow there were several hours of darkness, and that something might be due to happen before daylight.

Once I'd admitted the thought I couldn't rest. I slipped out of my room, closed the door softly behind me, and felt my way carefully along the wall and round the corner of the corridor to Crispin's room, next door. At our end of the passage it was intensely dark, like walking through

swathes of black velvet. Just for a moment the opening of
my door must have allowed a faint grey softening of the
darkness to become visible, enough to give warning to
someone who was already afoot before me there. I caught a
rapid and infinitely light rushing of feet, a sound one felt
as a vibration rather than heard. But it was positive enough
to have direction. It began at Crispin's door, and it fled
along the corridor towards the rear of the house. I heard
a latch click, and then silence. The disturbed air quivered
back to me faintly scented. Dorothy !

I felt my way to the panelled door that seemed now to
be warm and fragrant from her touch, as though she had
rested her cheek against the wood. My heart felt heavy as
lead. I was continually forgetting to allow for that possibility. What if Crispin had been only too right about her,
after all ? What if she was in her husband's murder up to
the neck, and now that her partner had arrived with the
news of Crispin's declaration of war, she had no choice but
to lend herself to the campaign against her son ? Too far
in to turn back, too inextricably committed to her lover's
side to be able to struggle back even as far as neutrality. If
that were conceivable—but of course it wasn't !—then what
more likely than that she should be the one delegated to try
and coax information out of the boy, to spy on him, to
watch his every move in the hope that he would lead her
to what he had hidden ?

No use suggesting that he should lock his door. He was
waiting for someone to open it. I tried it, easing the knob
round gingerly so that it gave without a sound, and pushed
the door gradually open until I could slide through into the
room. From the faintly luminous rectangle of the open
window a strong, cool draught blew over me, flaunting the
curtains half across the room.

" Crispin ! " I said in a level whisper.

No answer. The bed took shape in what light there was,

so bland and neat that there could not be anyone in it. It was not my business to be stealthy, I had every reason to emphasise my presence here, and Crispin's probable resentment no longer mattered. So I reached up a hand and switched on the light.

He was standing pressed against the wall, close to the window, the curtain blowing across his shoulder. His head was braced back, his hands well down in the pockets of his dressing-gown. His eyes, enormously dilated in the second before they reacted to the light, were fixed unwaveringly upon me, and continued so, unblinking, while his brows contracted into a protective frown, and his lids sank a little to shield his pupils. The lines of his face looked translucently white and hard, and his jaw was set so fiercely that it must have ached when he unclamped it.

" No," I said, " sorry ! It's only me ! "

" Are you trying to frighten me ? " he asked, with a rigid little smile ; and though he moved away from his strategic position, he did so with an elaborate unconcern which somehow made it clear that his knees were shaking slightly under him. He took his left hand out of his pocket, and pushed back his brown hair nervously from his forehead. I noticed he didn't withdraw his right hand, nor did the tension of his right arm relax completely.

" Quite the reverse," I said. " Trying to reassure myself. I just wanted to know that you were all right." And I offered him a cigarette, and watched with interest how he hesitated, and then shook his head firmly. It doesn't inevitably take two hands to light a cigarette, but men with two hands and both free habitually employ both on the job. Crispin's right hand wasn't free, and he didn't wish to be involved in any activities which might make the fact only too plain.

" Put the light out," he said, turning half away from me towards the window. " And come and look here."

I switched out the light and crossed to his side. He was

looking out across the wide expanse of lawns and flower-beds that ran very gently downhill towards the belt of trees that surrounded the garden, and separated it from the road. The drive made a broad ribbon of lambent light with its rosy gravel, plunging away from the front door, beneath us, to the gate, which was hidden beyond the trees.

" Look down there under the chestnut tree." He had edged well to the right, but it was to his right-hand side I came, all the same ; and when he pointed down into the garden, I leaned towards him to follow the direction more closely, and pressed myself, not too obtrusively, against his hip and arm. Every muscle in his arm was braced taut ; the hand in his pocket was a small, bony fist, all knuckles, clenched upon something compact and hard. A strongly right-handed boy using his left to point something out is in any case a sufficiently odd circumstance. He flinched at my touch, and drew very slightly, very carefully away from me, until we did no more than brush sleeves.

Under the chestnut tree near the drive, just within the main gate, darkness and dark greyness and relative light lay in a still and settled pattern, and at first gave away nothing to my eyes. Then, even without the aid of movement, for one instant I managed to assemble the vague design of the dark into the shape of a man. That stable oval of pallor was undoubtedly a face, raised and alert and fixed upon the house. I remembered that the light had been switched on for a few moments in this room, and could hardly doubt where the watcher's attention was focused now. Window space in the Lawns was lavish enough to have shown him clearly the two figures in the room. Making a guess at the angle, I thought it very likely that he had seen me with my finger on the switch the instant the light went on. Good, so it must be established in at least one interested head that I conferred with Crispin secretly after midnight. That suited me. And even the fact that we'd reverted to darkness so promptly fitted in admirably with the general illusion I was anxious to create.

The only thing was that this man ought not to have been there. He was a complication we couldn't afford. It would easily be possible for Crane or Keyes to leave the house by night and station himself under Crispin's window, but where was the point? Nor did this shadow seem to me to bulk like either of them. It was extremely tall, and its stillness seemed rather a physical quality than an effort of will. But the distance was considerable, and there was no certainty of outlines in all that gradation of greys and blacks, and every impression we gained of the half-glimpsed figure might be delusive.

" How long has he been there? " I asked.

" I saw him first a quarter of an hour or so before you came in. He was moving along through the trees, very slowly. Then I lost him completely, and just before you came I spotted him there, where he is now."

" Looking for the right window? " I suggested.

" I don't know." He was profoundly disturbed, his voice shook with tension, even restrained to a whisper as it was. He had the whole drama reduced to a bare simplicity of character and action, involving no more than four people in all, and but for the duplication of the initial " D " there would have been only three. And suddenly everything he had planned was disrupted, all his reasoning thrown into confusion, by the appearance of an unknown fifth.

Or was he unknown? Crispin's strained concentration puzzled me a little. He stared, and blinked, and shook his head, trying to make his eyes do miracles. And he gnawed his lip in an agony of uncertainty.

" Who is he? " I asked.

" I don't know."

" Are you sure? He means something to you."

" No—yes, I feel as though he ought to, and yet—

honestly, Evelyn, I don't know. If only I could see him better, but he's only a shadow now. It was when he was moving—you know how movements can be familiar, even in the dark. But if I ought to know him, I still can't place him. All I know is, he can't be here by chance, he must be something to do with this business. Why else should he be scouting round our house at one o'clock in the morning ? "

The shadow among the shadows hadn't moved, showed no intention of moving.

" Stay here in the window," I said, " and keep an eye on him. I'll be back."

I slipped down the stairs and out into the garden by the kitchen door, which put the entire house between me and the watcher among the trees. It wasn't difficult to reach the shrubberies without once advancing into the open, and once among the trees my chance of moving unobserved was as good as his. The night air was still and mild, and very quiet, but Dorothy's well-kept grass swallowed up footsteps like a layer of sponge rubber. I reached the drive, on the opposite side from the stranger, and crossed it flattened against the gate. There must be less than twenty-five yards between us now.

And then I had to step within a couple of feet of a brace of partridges, and they went off like rockets, filling the night with the whirring of their wings. There were trees between my quarry and me, I can't claim that I saw anything of his retreat. There wasn't much to hear, either, just a rapid rustling of branches and slithering of leaves, and then the scraping of shoe-toes against the wall.

I dived for the wall, too, crashing recklessly between the trees. A humpbacked shadow heaved itself up against the faint pallor of the sky, clear of the high parapet. I clawed at a flailing leg, closed my grip on his ankle, and pulled him toppling down again with a crackling of twigs and a heavy thud into the grass, but his heel caught me hard in the temple as I jumped from under him, and made my vision blur for a moment. I felt and heard his movements rather than saw them. He fell expertly, already gathering himself for the rebound, and rolling on knees and shoulders like an acrobat, took me round the knees and brought me down beside him. We threshed together in the grass, painfully locked, feeling for a damaging hold. It was dark down there, too dark to take note even of shapes and movements ; but what I felt of him were long hard arms like whalebone, and a strength and speed I doubted if I could match for long. He felt as tall as he'd looked, standing there under the trees, and there wasn't an ounce of fat on him. I would be winded before he was.

I got the heel of my hand under his jaw, and shoved him off with a thrust that wouldn't have done him much damage or me much good if the back of his head hadn't happened to make contact pretty sharply with the bole of a beech tree. It knocked him silly for no more than a second, but it gave me time to heave myself out of his grip and leap to my feet. He was whirling on his knees to reach me again when I grabbed the shoulders of his jacket, and dragged it down backwards to pin his arms to his sides. That, at least, was the idea, but he flung himself sideways, and my left hand lost its grip, and clawed its way down to lock in his inside pocket. Pocket and lining together tore away bodily as we struggled. I felt a pen snap through and spill ink over my fingers, and heard coins clash briefly before they rolled silently into the grass. He heaved himself clear and left a long, torn pennant of lining in my hand, and something larger and heavier than coins flew past my face and clanged against the tree.

My balance lost, I was spilled with the rest ; and before I could brace a foot under me and spring up again he had swung his right fist blindly at my jaw, a punch that lifted

me clean off the ground and laid me sprawling in the roots
of the beech. Something sharp stung my cheek, something
that rolled away from the impact. I tried to get up again,
but my bones were all as limp as the long shred of rag trailing
from my helpless hand. I was heaving gently up and down
on the surface of consciousness, like a cork on a playful sea,
sometimes submerged, sometimes buoyant, no sooner
clutching at restored sense than I was down again in the
trough. And he didn't wait to argue the toss further. Not
even to pick up his money. It would have taken him some
minutes to find the scattered coins, but one thing he'd
dropped was more easily discovered, and that was the one
thing he wanted.

The stabbing beam of a small torch leaped out of the
dark, and swept across the ground to my face, searching
the grass. It hurt, and, finding my head too heavy to lift,
I rolled my cheek deeper into the grass to escape from the
light. The grass blades stood out as sharp and broad as
swords ; and close to my dazed eyes lay something strange,
a shape of metal curled half round like curving wings, dull-
coloured but with gleams of brightness. The spiral lines
coiling over it made my eyes blur again, just as I registered
the certainty that it was this sharp, curved edge which had
punctured my cheek.

When I managed to open my eyes again it was to catch
one rapid glance of a lean hand and wrist, flashing down
out of the darkness to snatch the thing from the grass. I saw
it with that peculiar, exaggerated clarity things have in
close-up when the brain has temporarily lost its command of
the eyes. The dark hairs on the back of the hand stood out
so distinctly that they seemed to prick me, and the squat,
square nails at the ends of the sinewy fingers were like spades.
Across the wrist there was a short, puckered scar, faintly
brown. The hand gathered the metal band out of the turf,
and vanished, as the torch was switched off.

I heard the light thud of his landing on the other side of the wall, a few long, running steps, then silence. I lay wallowing for some seconds more in my painless daze, and then my head and my jaw began to ache wickedly, and I came slowly and angrily back to full consciousness. I braced my arms under me, and they'd recovered their bones. I'd had him in my hands and let him get away. The night was silent enough now, except for the pounding in my ears. Disgustedly I crawled to my feet, and went and dragged myself laboriously to the top of the wall ; but the road outside was empty and pallid in the silence.

I slid down the wall again clumsily, and stood leaning against it until my legs ceased to wilt under me. My brain wasn't working very well yet, it took some minutes for the glimpses printed on my eyes to eat their way through like acid into my mind, and sting hell out of the sensitive spots of memory there. When the gall of recollection and pain did penetrate, I dug my nails into the bricks of the wall and swore aloud.

A metallic shape like a bird with curved wings, engraved with the labyrinthine spirals of eternity. A long, sinewy hand outstretched to snatch it out of the grass, exposing for a moment a scarred brown wrist. I'd seen them both before, the one only in my mind's eye, the other in the quiet darkness of a London street, stretched downwards beside mine in that identical gesture as he reached to pick up Dorothy's dropped book. I'd had my hands on both the man and the mask, and let them both slip through my fingers !

Not Dermot. Not David. This inexplicable stranger, seen once, just once, lean and dark and silent, emerging from a deserted doorway and walking away at an even pace along the street and into darkness again, with that one long, disquieting, significant look at Dorothy as he passed. I knew nothing about him, he had no name, no identity, there was no place for him in the puzzle, unless Crispin could suggest one. But he had the mask! Only one person could have the mask, and that was the murderer.

I remembered the tearing cloth, and the shower of coins, and dropped to my knees to grope round in the grass, but without a light it was hopeless trying to find anything there. Besides, I must go back to Crispin, or he'd come looking for me. And was I going to tell him everything that had happened? Better not. If I meant to take the affair out of his hands to-morrow, why add fuel to the fire to-night? Let him go on waiting confidently for his expected visitor. If he suspected that I was deflecting the pursuit in my own direction there was no guessing what desperate, irrevocable things he might not do to keep his feud in his own hands.

When I crept up the stairs again, after washing my face and tidying myself up hurriedly in the downstairs cloakroom, my eyes were used to the darkness, and as I entered his room I needed no light to see Crispin withdrawing his hand smartly but with creditable coolness and neatness from under his pillow. He covered the movement by smoothing at the already smooth covers of the bed, and turned to face me without a quiver.

" What happened? Did you get a look at him? "

" Depends what you call a look," I said. " It's darker than pitch under those trees. I had a slight brush with him, but he got away over the wall. We shan't see any more of him to-night."

He saw the fresh ooze of blood along the cut on my cheek, and his eyes grew wide. " Are you hurt? Did he have a knife? "

" No, it's nothing. We tangled under the wall, and he knocked me silly and cleared out. I'm all right—just annoyed with myself, that's all."

" You didn't get any idea what he's like? You didn't know him? "

"Tall, thin, tough—that's about all I can say. He certainly isn't anyone from the house, Crispin—neither Crane nor Keyes."

"No," said Crispin, his voice querulous with bewilderment and sleepiness and anxiety, "I realised that." He dropped his head into his hands to stifle a huge yawn.

"Yes. You'd better go to bed," I said, "where you ought to have been long ago. There's nothing more we can do now. All I intended to do was look in and make sure you were all right, not start a manhunt."

When he stood up, with remarkable docility for him, and began to slip off his dressing-gown, I was quick to relieve him of it and throw it over the back of the chair beside his bed. There was nothing small, hard and heavy in the right-hand pocket now, which didn't surprise me.

"If you need me," I said, "I'm next door, you've only to call me."

From his pillow he suddenly gave me a tired, melting smile, and visibly abandoned everything until morning. "Good night, Evelyn!" he said.

"Good night, Crispin!"

I, on the contrary, had still something to do before I slept. I consider I did it rather neatly. At any rate, he never noticed anything odd about my exit, nor heard me whisk out the key from his side of the lock as I passed. I closed the door on him quietly, and gave him five minutes to fall at least half asleep before I risked locking him in. Fortunately Dorothy's staff kept everything in first-class order, and the key turned in the wards almost without a sound, as smoothly as silk.

After that I went down again, very quietly, to the trampled circle of grass under the garden wall, and searched it inch by inch with a torch. The torn strip of greasy and threadbare grey lining told me nothing, except that his coat had been in wear for a good many years. The mask, far too big for an inside breast pocket, must have been carried between jacket and lining for safety. The fountain-pen that had snapped like a thin bone in my grip I never did find, maybe it had remained dangling by its clip from the corner of pocket I'd left him. But I found six coins in all. A florin, a sixpence, one penny and two halfpennies. The sixth was considerably more interesting ; it was a Greek drachma.

CHAPTER XII

I UNLOCKED Crispin's door at dawn, and opened it just wide enough to slip the key into the lock on the inner side again. Luckily he slept through the operation, his nose burrowing into the pillow, his one visible cheek soft and flushed under the tousled brown hair, his lips parted and dewy as a baby's. Completely off-guard, his appearance was innocent and charming ; or so I thought, until I observed that his hand was thrust under the pillow, and no doubt still locked on the butt of the pistol he'd so carefully kept out of my sight the previous night. On what particular part of his person he'd smuggled that item through the Customs was just one of the things he hadn't told me.

By daylight my whole instinct was to take the thing firmly away from him, smack his behind, and read him an irate lecture on the iniquity of small boys who play with firearms. Even the childishness of this traditional hiding-place contributed to the impression that he was about ten years old, rather than an overburdened and precocious sixteen. But it was quite useless, at this late stage, to begin treating him as a juvenile, who had no right to be running his own affairs. He might, with luck, be outwitted without being outraged, but he'd fight me to the death rather than be dispossessed of the load he carried on the grounds that he was too young to be trusted with it. And the pistol was a symbol. Bruce's, no doubt; I wondered what kind of gun Bruce had favoured, and whether Crispin had also been so thoughtful as to bring home the licence with it. And whether he carried it on him during the day, as well as keeping it ready to hand at night.

He would have to be separated from it, of course, but preferably not too roughly. If one more night could settle the whole business, then Crispin might very well sleep through the crisis just as serenely as he'd slept through the indignity of being locked in.

He slept late, and came down to breakfast a little drunk still with sleep, and more than a little cross. In confronting those he suspected of being his enemies, his sense of fitness demanded that he should be polite and ceremonious, though he couldn't bring himself to be gracious. The more absolute the enmity, the more superb would Crispin's manners be. But I was the nearest thing he had to an intimate, and towards me he could afford to be ill-tempered to the point of rudeness. He wasn't going to like my defensive tactics, either, since he had no desire whatever to be defended from solitary combat with his enemy. I was prepared for a difficult day; I was even ready to wring some perverse enjoyment out of it.

David Keyes had to go into Wells that morning, Saturday, and collect his motor-bike, which it seemed the garage had promised to have ready for him by ten. Crane promptly offered to drive him in in the Austin, and invited Crispin to accompany them.

" We could have a look at the cathedral together," he said, watching Crispin across the table, " and then have lunch somewhere in the town before we drive home."

And that, I thought, would leave just two of you to drive back in the Austin, not to mention the ever-ready solitudes of a great cathedral. And I could see Crispin thinking the

same. His head went up alertly; his eyes were suddenly
clear and wild. He opened his lips to accept at once, gladly
and fiercely. It must have been agony waiting for the
first move in the game; and if this was it, he welcomed
it.

"Why don't we take the Jaguar, and all go?" I said,
turning to Dorothy.

She jumped at it. "Yes, let's! It's a lovely day, and I
do want to do some shopping. We'll all meet for lunch
somewhere in town, and David can convoy us home."

David didn't seem to mind. Crispin veiled his eyes, after
one bitterly speculative glance at me, and kept his feelings
to himself. Crane frowned, but could not object; and his
control of his features was at all times too civilised and
severe for anger or uneasiness to show.

So we all went to Wells. I drove there, but once in town,
Dorothy took over the car for her shopping. By all the rules
I ought to have offered to pilot her expedition, do the
carrying for her, and cope with the tedious difficulties of
Saturday parking, but I didn't. It was Crane who drew
his handsome dark brows together austerely, and suggested
that it would be convenient and helpful if someone stayed
with her; by which he certainly did not mean himself.
And Dorothy, knowing nothing of the weight she was lifting
from my mind, laughed at him, and said she preferred
shopping alone, thank you, she wanted no bored and suffering male sitting outside shops with a martyred air, studying
his watch every few minutes. Especially as she'd telephoned
for a dress fitting as soon as we'd made up our minds to
come, and was liable to be out of circulation most of the
morning. She promised to meet us for lunch at half past
twelve, and drove off and left us to our sight-seeing.

David having gone off to his garage, we three who
remained duly toured the cathedral. It was a morose
morning. Wherever we went, there was I in between the

two of them. I suspect I did more than my share of the talking. As long as I was there, nothing of moment could be said, and the marked silence of non-appreciation had to be filled in somehow. Crane did talk across me, so far as that was possible, but it was uphill work, and the conversation resolved itself into one of those distressing question-and-answer affairs which cause boys such agonies of resentment and fury—the " well-how-are-you-getting-on-at-school " persuasion, except that in Crispin's case it wasn't a question of school. Against a barrage of mono-syllables from the victim, each one dryer and more grudging than the last, Crane couldn't help sounding every moment more insufferably patronising, while Crispin muttered into his collar, and chafed, and flushed, like any one of the schoolboy species he so despised. If this was the beginning of the battle, it wasn't turning out at all as he'd led himself to expect. He took refuge within himself, and studied to keep his footing as an adult by reverting to his old tone of sophisticated insolence, but its veneer of indulgent polite-ness sounded ominously cracked, and the general effect was of adolescent cheek, which was not at all what he was aiming at. If we're wrong about Crane, I remember thinking, and he's on the level, what a brat he'll think Bruce's boy has developed into.

By the time we turned thankfully towards the hotel where we were to meet Dorothy, we'd sunk even lower, and were at the I-hope-you're-a-good-boy-to-your-mother stage, and Crispin's mortification, as touching in its way as his hand under the pillow gripping the machinery of life and death, had drawn me right back into the horrors of adolescence, which I'd forgotten for years. Indignity and anti-climax were all the morning had to offer him. On the whole, I thought the change might be good for him ; he was being scaled down nicely to size. For whole minutes together I could almost forget that he'd ever appeared to me as moving in a monstrous thundercloud of antique tragedy, with death looking over his shoulder.

It wouldn't last, of course, I knew that. The sun might be shining on the streets, but the invisible shadow of Agamemnon still lay heavy on us.

Dorothy drove up ten minutes late, and with a great many parcels piled in the back seat. She looked beautiful, and vague, and every inch a woman after her session at the dressmaker's, with the brightness and satisfaction of a child who has played all morning with attractive toys. I hadn't seen her look like that since I'd met her again in London, and even now this extreme radiance had an ephemeral look about it, and an odd quality of ruefulness, as if she herself knew all the time that it was slipping out of her hold. She stepped out of the car and sailed across the pavement with that wonderful thoroughbred walk of hers, her head back, her violet eyes, under their plaintive, lofty brows, dwelling in astonished tenderness on Crispin. Even more than the rest of the world, it appeared, he could never fail to fill her with wonder. Every first glimpse of him, even after a separation only a few hours long, caused her to start and quiver, as though she marvelled that this creature so remote and unapproachable, balanced against her in an apparently irreconcilable enmity, could be a child of her own flesh. She seemed first to spring towards him, and then to halt, frustrated, against the wall of glass that shut them apart.

We lunched, but it wasn't a success. David chattered, either impervious to the uneasiness of those about him, or labouring under an exaggerated sense of duty ; but he was the only one with much to say for himself. He had his motor-bike back again, and was happy. It suddenly occurred to me to wonder what I should do if he invited Crispin to ride back to Chilcot Mendip on the pillion. I could hardly prevent Crispin from jumping at the offer, as he was almost certain to do, and quite certainly no third person could insinuate himself between them there. But David, if he had any desire to cut Crispin out from the flock, was too subtle to go about it that way. We four drove back to the Lawns in the Jaguar, and David followed alone. He intended, he said, to call in at Chilcot Mendip, where there were said to be some excellent brasses in the church.

He didn't come in until tea-time. I had stuck closely to Crispin's elbow all day, and he was chafing badly by that time, so that he looked almost pleased to see David loping across the lawn towards our group of chairs. Dorothy reached for another cup, and poured tea. Crispin kicked the stay firmly into its slots in the back of another chair, and David dropped into it, blown and rosy, and quite incredibly boyish. I always found his youthfulness too good to be true.

" The most amazing thing ! I caught sight of an old acquaintance of ours to-day, Dermot——"

" In Wells ? " asked Dermot.

" No, here, in Chilcot Mendip. The last person in the world I'd have expected to see here. He didn't see me, and by the time I'd pulled in and parked the bike I'd lost him, so I'm no nearer knowing what on earth he can be doing in England——"

Dermot sat up abruptly in his chair, his brows drawing together. " Who was it ? "

" You'll never guess ! Stavros Diakos !."

Crispin was in the act of handing David's tea. The cup chattered and sang suddenly in the saucer, and tipped over, shedding hot tea over Crispin's hand and David's sleeve. The boy drew back with a start and an indrawn breath, and righted the cup with a hand that was shaking visibly.

" Oh lord, I'm sorry ! I can't think how I did that. Clumsy oaf I must be ! "

He hurriedly put down the cup to mop agitatedly at David's sleeve, his face alternately paling and flushing under our eyes. I'd never seen him so disconcerted ; and certainly clumsiness was something new in Crispin, and might be expected to dismay him out of all proportion. But all his unwonted energy in scolding himself and making apologies for his inadequacy couldn't conceal, from me at least, that it was the name which had shattered him, not the accident.

David shrugged it off good-humouredly. " Don't fuss, Cris, it's quite all right, no harm done."

" I'll get you another cup," said Crispin, and by force of will held this one still as he handed it. When he sat down again I noticed that he had turned his chair a little, so that none of us looked directly at him, and in a moment he fished out his sun-glasses and put them on. They restored to his face a certain synthetic calm ; but I was between him and the others, and I could see the silent rapidity of his breathing, and the irresolution of his quivering lip, until he caught it in his teeth. Not just surprise ; something more than that, retrospective recognition. Our midnight visitor was identified. No wonder his movements had been familiar to Crispin's eye, and caused him so much wretched uneasiness.

" Stavros Diakos ? What, Bruce's foreman ? " Dermot lay back in his chair, but did not, I noticed, relax. " Sure you're not making a mistake ? I only left him in Pirithoön a month ago, why on earth should he be here ? He was going after some job in Athens, he asked me for a reference —and I heard from his wife he got the job, too. What would be likely to bring him to England ? You must be seeing things ! "

" Stavros, I assure you." David was enjoying his sensation. " I don't know any more than you do what he's doing here, but he's here all right. He was standing outside a shop in Market Street, near the square. By the time it had registered, and I'd parked in the square and walked back to look for him, he was gone. I wandered round the town for a bit, thinking I might see him again, but I didn't. But take it from me, it was Stavros."

And now it was anybody's guess who was dissembling, and who wasn't. Was Dermot really as surprised as he seemed ? For the matter of that, was David ? Were there two people working together in the affair, and if so, which two ? And Dorothy, where did she fit in ? Had Dorothy and her hypothetical lover employed Stavros in the affair ? I contemplated any solution involving Dorothy always with a sense of shock and disbelief, but I had to allow for everything.

Dorothy herself sat there silent behind the tea-tray, looking questioningly from face to face, her brow clouded. There was no seeing into the mind behind those great eyes of hers. Only the boy, where this one issue was concerned, was crystal to me. He sat drawn together defensively into himself, hooding his eyes behind the dark glasses, but his fingers gripped nervously round the arms of his chair, and there was a dew of sweat on his upper lip. If he relaxed his rigidity for a moment he would be trembling in reaction. Crispin had thought the world of Stavros, who had treated him like an extra son. Of all the people round him at Pirithoön, Stavros was the only one in whom he might have brought himself to confide. He couldn't bear that Stavros should be involved in Bruce's death. Whoever it was, it mustn't be Stavros ! Crispin's heart would break if it turned out that way.

When I looked at him I almost forgot, in my ache for him, the agony of indecision and anxiety I felt over Dorothy.

CHAPTER XIII

I WENT INTO Crispin's room just before midnight, when the
house had been quiet for long enough to make any movements noticeable, while at the same time absolving them
from too prompt suspicion of being intended for notice.
Not even the innocent would yet be sound asleep. Crispin
certainly would not. He had too much on his mind.

This time he was prepared for me, though ready, too, in
case after all it should be the other visitor he still expected.
He was in bed, propped up among his pillows, and from
under them, I observed, he withdrew his right hand as I
came in. His bedside lamp was still burning, or else he had
switched it on when he heard my hand at the door. He
watched me cross the room to him with a brooding face.

I sat down on the chair beside his bed, and asked him
directly : " What's all this about Stavros Diakos ? "

" You heard as much as I did," said Crispin coldly.

" Stavros was your man rather than anybody else's. You
didn't know he was in England ? "

" I didn't know anything about him, since the day I left
Pirithoön, until David said that this afternoon. Even now
I don't know it's true."

The whispers of our voices, low and rapid, made a
rustling of breath in the room, and the stillness of the night
took it and magnified it. I wondered if we had a watcher
under the trees to-night, perhaps more than one. They
ought to be given a glimpse of my silhouette at the window,
against this admirable small light it would be effective for
identification purposes.

I got up and crossed to the window, which stood wide
open on the warm night, with curtains drawn well back.

" I think you do," I said. " It was Stavros you saw down there last night, wasn't it ? You couldn't place him then, but you knew well enough who it was, as soon as David mentioned the name. Didn't you ? "

Crispin said : " No ! " making such a painful gulp at the lie that I wanted to go over and pat his back to help it up.

" Have it your own way. What sort of man is this Stavros ? Has he travelled ? Would he be likely to turn up in England ? "

" No," repeated Crispin in a violent whisper, " why should he ? He *has* travelled, he spent several years in the United States when he was a young man. He speaks good English, and he's quite competent to go wherever he likes. But why should he come here ? There's nothing to bring him here."

" There's you," I suggested gently.

" If he'd wanted to keep in touch with me he'd have written. No, he was very good to me while we were all there together, he liked me, but when it was finished it would just be finished. His life's in Pirithoön, and mine's moved here. I didn't expect him to write to me. Why should he ? And why on earth should he just set out and come here, without saying a word ? Why, it would probably cost him everything he had."

" In that case, you think someone else must have paid his fare ? In other words, he's become somebody else's man ? "

Heaven knows I didn't want to torment him ; but I did want to find out what was going on in his mind, while I waited for the soft, penetrating sound of our whispering voices to reach the ears of all those within the house who might be interested, as the glimmer of our light had surely reached any watchers outside.

" He's his own man," said Crispin haughtily, " and always was. But I don't believe he's here at all. Either

David made that tale up for some purpose of his own, or else he saw somebody rather like Stavros, that's all. Stavros is in Greece, and I'm not such a fool as to believe anything else."

" Then who was it you saw and almost recognised last night ? "

" I don't know. But it wasn't Stavros," he said, setting his chin like a bulldog, and glaring at me desperately across his drawn-up knees.

" My dear Crispin, it wasn't just the mention of his name that upset you so much this afternoon. It was the fact that as soon as David said it, it rang a bell with you. You knew at once who it was you'd seen in the garden."

" No ! " he cried passionately, " I didn't ! It was only a shock hearing David say he was here, but I realised almost at once it couldn't be true."

" You're not cut out for a liar," I said sympathetically, shaking my head over his inadequacy.

He didn't pour out any more protests or denials, but heaved himself round in the tangle of bedclothes and turned his back on me. " If you don't want to believe me, I'm not interested in arguing," he said, and pointedly settled down in his bed, stretching himself out with a sigh.

" All right," I said resignedly, dredging my brains for something comforting to say to him, " you didn't see him, there was nobody in the garden, he's in Greece, where you left him. But don't forget a man can move from place to place unobtrusively for good motives, as well as bad ones. No need to write Stavros off too soon." I was thankful he couldn't know how disingenuous that was. He knew nothing about the sharp-edged wing that had cut my face.

" Good night, Crispin ! "

He let me get to the door, and then he melted suddenly, and I heard the young, warm, tentative voice of his most vulnerable moments : " Good night, Evelyn ! "

I went back to my own room, and completed the stuffing of a large brief-case with parcels wrapped carefully in wadding and brown paper, and sealed down as was fitting for something as precious as gold. The parcels were shaped as nearly as possible to accord with Crispin's descriptions of the pieces he had found. Dorothy's garage had provided a good many of the scraps of metal which did duty as pectoral plates and masks, and some old, ornate and exceedingly ugly curtain rings from the attic served as armlets and bracelets. I had no way of knowing how nearly my treasure approximated to the original in bulk and quantity, but then, the man who wanted it so badly had never seen the original, either, except in his mind's dazzled eye. The collection I'd amassed just went into the brief-case when tightly packed, distorting it monstrously, but still allowing it, with difficulty, to be closed, strapped and locked. When finished, the decoy weighed encouragingly heavy, and looked convincingly bulky and important. This was an operation certainly not intended for any eyes but my own. The curtains were drawn close over it, and the only light I used was a minute pocket lamp. If a thread of light under the door suggested some nocturnal activity on my part, well and good, provided it didn't furnish a clue to what I was up to at that moment.

I changed into old flannels, a dark sweater, and rubber-soled shoes. It was then about half past twelve, and I had still one more thing to do before I could set out. Twice I stole out and listened at Crispin's door, and each time I thought I could catch faint sounds of stirrings in the bed. The third time all was absolutely still. I coaxed the door open, and still nothing moved within. Then I could hear, as I strained my ears into the darkness, the long, soft, sleeping breaths heave and fall, very quietly, very serenely. He was deep asleep, relaxed and at rest just as I had left him, his back turned to the door. He had fallen asleep without turning again, without sliding a hand upwards to reassure himself that his armoury was still intact.

Robbing him wasn't so difficult, after all. He had rolled himself to the far edge of the pillow, and I was able to slip my hand underneath and draw out the pistol in one long, smooth movement, without disturbing him. I hadn't been mistaken, a pistol it was. It lay in my palm snug and warm from its hiding-place. And I wasn't in the least proud of my dexterity in lifting it from him, but I was indescribably glad to think that he could no longer make use of it to saddle himself with the commission of some act which could never be undone. Moreover, I needed it, at this moment, more than he did. Guns are things I don't habitually carry, and they're not easy to get hold of at short notice.

Crispin slept on peacefully, fathoms deep from the world and his own inescapable troubles. I crept away gingerly, but he never stirred. I'd intended to make doubly sure of his rest by locking him in again, in case my decoy failed to draw the enemy, but this time I met with a setback, for the key wasn't in the lock. There was no time left for wondering who had removed it, though the most probable person was certainly Crispin himself. Maybe, after all, he hadn't slept through my manœuvre of yesterday. I looked back at the slender figure in the bed, listened to the deep, easy, relaxed breathing, and couldn't believe he was pretending. If that wasn't genuine, then I was a Dutchman.

In my own room, by torchlight, I had a look at the gun. It was a small German-made automatic, no doubt picked up by Bruce somewhere in the Middle East ; I wasn't familiar with it, and didn't care to risk putting on the light to examine it more closely, but it seemed to be a small-calibre job, probably .300. Quite enough to kill, if used at short range even by a beginner. It was fully loaded. I felt better about the meanness of my theft after I'd checked on that.

Now at least he was deprived of the means of committing murder; and the rest was up to me.

I slipped down the stairs with my brief-case under my arm, unbolted the french doors in the garden-room, and let myself out on to the terrace. It was an ideal night for man-hunting, not too light, not too dark, not complicated with the sharp shadows and glaring brilliance of a moon, not noisy with wind, yet not quite still. Sounds would carry well in that air, and yet avoid the implication that only somebody who wanted to be followed would be afoot on such a night on secret business. I went through all the motions of stealth, sliding along the wall of the house, darting across the open forecourt at the narrowest possible spot and burying myself in the belt of bushes, halting under the nearest tree for a few minutes, flattened against the trunk to cast no separate shadow in the soft, faded luminosity of the stars, while I looked back at the house to make sure I wasn't followed. Or to make sure that I was.

No one would be fool enough to walk on the drive if he wanted to pass unheard and unseen; but in slipping from tree to tree over a wide space of grass to avoid an open drive, a man can make his very furtiveness obtrusive. Sudden rapid bursts of movement, however silent, disturb the air of the night with a vibration which I've often thought must carry for miles. I made no more halts until I was in the trees close to the gate. It wouldn't do to be too obviously preoccupied with pursuit, once I was clear of the house. I strained my ears then, and could detect nothing in the way of a step, the brushing of leaves, anything to indicate that I was followed. There remained, however, the other as yet untested possibility, that there might once again be watchers somewhere in the grounds who would rise to the bait, and pick up my trail as I passed them.

There was a small swing gate beside the carriage gates, well shadowed by the overhanging branches of a chestnut

tree. Like everything about the Lawns, it was admirably
kept, and made not a sound when I slid round it and out
on to the road. A wide footpath ran alongside the garden
wall, and the trees leaning over afforded deeper shadow,
and confused the air with the faint stirrings by which trees
converse at night in all weathers, except perhaps in the
ominous stillness before a storm. I hugged the wall, and
went ahead in a fast, light walk, knowing that the very
small sounds I made must be perfectly clear to anyone
following, and therefore afraid to halt here or even slacken.
Once off the road and back on grass I could afford to pause
in cover and look back ; and there, too, on that long, open
slope, my pursuer—supposing I had scored at least one
pursuer by now—would be more exposed than I should, as
well as less acquainted with such cover as did exist there.
What I mustn't do was to be too clever about leaving the
road again. The last thing I wanted was to shake him, if I'd
drawn him.

I hadn't far to go on the road. Beyond the garden of the
Lawns a row of motley semi-detacheds began, and beyond
them again there was a large new pub. Between these two
a narrow lane turned up towards the hills, dwindling into a
cart-track, then a sheep-track, as it left the buildings behind.
As soon as I turned the corner into the lane I halted against
the wall, for the sound of my steps would in any case be
cut off sharply by the turning. I couldn't risk looking back,
a flutter of movement there at the level of a man's face
might be only too noticeable, and I didn't know whether
I had him, or, if I had, how close to me he was. I could
only hold my breath, and listen.

Someone was there, all right ! There was no doubt of it
as soon as I myself was still. Hardly a perceptible step,
only the slight, regular, rustling contact of a shoe-sole with
the dry concrete of the path, the easing along of a man's
weight upon rubber soles just hard enough to grate against

that gritty texture. Something between a squeak and a
whisper, so infinitesimally soft that if the leaves had been
stirring then I shouldn't have caught it. But they were
still, and I heard. Too controlled, too stealthy a sound to
belong to an honest foot going home ; and besides, almost
instantly it quickened to a new tempo. I knew what that
meant. He had been near enough to me to see me turn into
the lane, and he didn't want me to get so far ahead that he
might lose me. The wall between us would cut off sound
enough to let him—— I realised abruptly that he'd broken
into a soft, long-stepping run, and instead of standing there
theorising about his move to gain on me and have me under
close observation, I turned and ran for it myself, going up
the lane for the first fifty yards like a scalded cat.

I had to keep my distance. For one thing, the showdown
had to be on my own ground, not in some fortuitous place
on the way which might favour him rather than me ; and
for another, he would expect me to feel satisfied now that
I was away from the house, and move smartly about this
nocturnal business of mine. And for the present I had to
do, or seem to be doing, what he expected. Too many
glances over my shoulder, and he'd begin to suspect that I
wanted him on my tail. He mustn't smell any rats yet.

I climbed the stile at the end of the cart-track, and took
to the scrambling, stony paths up the first slope, where no
man could hope to make his progress inaudible, and haste
would be more convincing than caution. Higher up there
was coarse, springy grass, tussocky and hard on the ankles,
but silent going unless it was too dry, and it wouldn't be.
The delicate, dimpled sheep-tracks went round and round
the contours, rising and dropping only by long, gradual
traverses here and there. I climbed up them as up a flight
of stairs, and emerged on the gentler, open slope above,
which was all grass. There was an outcrop of rocks somewhat to the right, the first cover on the hillside, and a few

trees, rustling faintly in the fresher breeze that made itself
felt up here, clear of the houses. I made for this spot, and
looked back from the shelter of the rocks, to make sure
that my shadow hadn't missed his way in that first complex
of tracks.

I was getting used to the darkness by now, and so must
he be. Outlines were easier to distinguish than they had
been, and the curious lambent light that picks out the
paler spots in any landscape by night mapped the bare
tracks for me very faintly, and made a shapeless pallor of
the occasional naked faces of limestone. Somewhere in the
vague darkness, clear of these paler forms, I was aware of
movement, of someone advancing now steadily, without
haste, up the hillside on my heels.

I didn't linger, once I was sure of him. If the interval
between us had shortened perceptibly when I moved into
his field of vision again he would begin to suspect that I
had my eye on him. I made a spurt with the bulk of the
rocks between us, and made good the yards I'd surrendered
before I veered left again, and steered for the long, rolling
crest above us, where already I could sense, though I
couldn't yet see, the hummock of the coppice against the
skyline.

From there on I didn't look back, but I slackened speed,
as though the slope had taken it out of me, and I had in
any case relaxed into a conviction of being utterly alone.
The entrance into the cave was going to be ticklish, and
needed accurate timing. On my hands and knees through
the rock archway, that was going to be a vulnerable moment.
Supposing he should be so sure of himself that he chose to
knock me on the head, or put a bullet in me, and tip me
down the shaft, instead of waiting to see what I did with
my burden? But on the whole I didn't seriously anticipate
that he'd kill if he could help it. Why should he, if he could
get what he wanted without the inconvenience of leaving a

corpse around ? If he was as convinced as I hoped he was that I had the gold under my arm, then he could hardly be in doubt that I'd brought it up here simply to hide it in what I took to be a safe place. And all he had to do was wait for me to go away, and then retrieve it. No mess, no subsequent manhunt, since the stuff was stolen anyhow, and we couldn't go to the police, nobody to turn up at some unexpected moment, no crime, no clues. What a fool he'd be to act too soon, and take all the unnecessary risks that would involve ! He who hides can find, they say. He who watches another fellow hide can find, too.

I was beginning to wonder whether I hadn't set him too stiff a course, considering he had to negotiate it in the dark, and without previous knowledge. I could hardly pretend to have heard nothing if he pitched head-first down the shaft on top of me. But it was too late to think of all the things that could come unstuck. They'd always been there in the design, they were no more likely now than before. And we were here, and couldn't turn back, even if we'd wished.

I crept through the trees, and stooped to the low, half-hidden opening of the shaft. And in case he had lost sight of me for a moment, or might be unable to locate precisely the spot where I entered the rock, I hit my head in stooping under the archway, and swore just once, in a furious under-tone that sounded like a shout to me. I let my toes scrabble along the stone as I crawled inside, so that he should be able to reconstruct even actions he couldn't see.

Then I was in the dark pocket within, feeling round for the edge of the shaft and the staples that anchored our ladder. I went down backwards, feeling for rung after rung with cautious toes, slowly, letting him hear me grunt, so that he'd know how the ground fell away. I'd done every-thing I could think of to get him inside there with me silently and safely, barring holding a torch for him while he made his way down ; and once I was in the gallery below, where we'd cached our dirty overalls and lights and ropes, I'd even do that, or something very like it.

I took my time in that first chamber, partly to make sure he was still on my trail, partly to let him get a good look at the ground below, and my activities. The first thing I did was to grope my way into our box of equipment, and fish out a small lamp, which I switched on and left burning there, close to the foot of the shaft. By the time I'd buckled on my belt, with our most powerful electric light strapped on to the front, and the brief-case hooked on at my left hip, I knew he was there above, crouching inside the entrance. I could hear faint movements of shoes and rustling of cloth as he gathered himself into stillness, then nothing, only the air inside there seemed to me to heave gently with his long, silent breathing. We weren't twenty-five feet apart now. I was just out of his line of vision, or so I calculated, but the light I had provided would show him the rope ladder, and the uneven rock floor below him, and prevent him from breaking his neck before I was ready to break it for him.

The big lamp on my belt I didn't switch on. That was for future use. Instead, I put on one of the miners' helmets we'd used on our first expedition here, and steered by the small light fixed to it, which was enough to show me my way and indicate to him where I was. I took a third light with me, too, a flat-based lamp that would stand on any reasonably flat surface. It had a handle, and hitched on to the belt without getting in my way. Then I slung a coil of thin rope over one shoulder and pushed on through the slippery, cold, ugly little chamber, dripping everywhere with water, into the big gallery beyond. I looked back just once, and saw the lower ends of the rope ladder stir and contort in their staples as he lowered his weight on to it, and that was all I needed to see.

Caves don't have any day or night, nothing but this cold, dank, enclosed darkness, oppressive and remote, that does away with all the times of day and all the seasons of the year. I felt the chill through my sweater, and hated the insecurity of my rubber-soled shoes on the slimy, whispering, watery floor, especially along the rim of the hole that dropped away to the lower gallery. But already I'd lost the sense of the small hours. The shadows that wavered along the rock walls from my lamp, streaming from every glistening, wet knob and every unevenness, were the same shadows as at noonday. And I was already as dirty as I should have been at noonday, fooling about here with Crispin.

I leaned over the neck of the inverted funnel, and felt the cold air surge up out of it and stiffen my cheeks. The distant sound of water came up, too, very curiously, cast from wall to wall in small, confused echoes from the underground stream far below. It was like listening to somebody in another room, mumbling in his sleep. Down below in the great gallery it would be like thunder, and send vibrations through the folds of the soiled, soapy rock.

Was he there with me yet ? I thought so ; I had a sense of his presence by that time, a prickling of the scalp, an awareness of eyes on me, not altogether unpleasant. There was plenty of cover up here, the walls of this gallery were complicated and broken, if he wanted to get close to me he could do it without much risk. The rising murmur of the water embraced all other small sounds and made them part of itself, at least until one's ears were accustomed to it. All the same, I heard him move, there at the distant end of the gallery, not once but three times, the mere stirring of cloth against slippery rock, and each time nearer. I looked all round me before I stooped to examine the knots that anchored our long ladder in its staples, which were made fast in a cleft, a yard back from the rim of the oubliette. The small light danced before me as I turned my head, snatching out of the dark a small, brilliant space of radiance, making rocks leap to life in an incredible minute clarity of detail, then casting them back into the obscurity. I had a feeling of the weight and solidity of the earth over my head, as neutral as the grave. Withdrawn from me, deep in blackness, a foot shifted, and was still.

The ladder was firm, the staples so placed in the cleft that the weight of a man dependent from them would only pull them farther in, not dislodge them. We'd made a good job of that. I hitched at my belt, and eased myself cautiously backwards over the edge of the rock, and on to the ladder.

The intense, dank cold welled up round me as though I'd lowered myself into icy water, and the long, glistening, ceaseless trickles of wet dripped on to my shoulders and head as soon as I had clambered downwards clear of the rim. I swung in air, because the walls of the cave expanded away from me in all directions now that I was through the neck of the bottle, behind me enormously, to the full great width of the lower gallery, before me to a distance of six feet or so on this upper part of the descent, though halfway down this wall closed in again, and we'd been able to make the ladder fast for a midway stage. For the last twenty feet or so the wall was smooth, glazed and sheer, and the ladder hung steady against it as against masonry, so that we hadn't bothered to anchor the foot, which dangled loose on the rock floor.

I went down hand over hand, rather clumsily, dangling lamp and rope and brief-case like a Christmas tree. I had gone about this whole descent with deliberation, to convey to him the impression that I was no longer on guard, but believed I had all the time in the world at my disposal, and was quite free of any watching eyes. For time was now something I had to fill up, while he made haste to overtake it. Somehow I had to make what I had to do outlast by a handsome margin his descent of the ladder after me, and provide enough movement and sound to cover it. Luckily the mere size of this enormous hall, and still more the roar of the water far below, almost took care of extraneous sound without any help from me.

I touched bottom, stepping down cautiously on to an undulating floor glistening with orange-brown deposits. The length of the hall, only a tiny segment of it lit by my helmet-lamp, receded into absolute darkness before me. On my right the great wall hung draped with curtains of slimy reddish deposits, fold on massive fold. On my left, for perhaps half the length of the hall, the opposite wall ran in a great sheer face of uncoated rock, and then fell back some six feet to arch over the roaring void at the bottom of which, unseen and unseeable, but filling the gulf with flying spray and moving air, the underground river crashed and cavorted through what sounded like a series of falls.

I hoped that my pursuer had followed my descent closely enough to have memorised the moves, and the ground immediately below ; I could hardly leave him a light at the foot to ensure his safe landing, but so far I couldn't complain of any incompetence on his part. My estimate of his way of thinking had so far proved pretty accurate, too, since he hadn't simply cut the ladder loose and let me fall forty feet or so on to the rock. He could have got his hands on the brief-case easily enough that way, just by helping himself to another rope from our store, but he would have had to face the remote possibility that some day someone would come caving, and find me. No, he was going to behave in a thoroughly sensible and restrained way, let me bury my treasure undisturbed and go away, and then, at leisure, he would dig it up again. If it proved to be what he hoped, then he would have gained it without giving away his identity or one point in the game ; and if by any chance it was a plant—did he entertain that suspicion ? I'd have given a lot to know !—then he had lost nothing, and stayed out of the trap, enlarging his knowledge of the opposition, and denying them any enlightenment about himself.

So I reasoned as I walked away from the ladder towards the gulf, and switched on my spare lamp, setting it on a smooth golden hummock near to the edge of the void. A few stalagmitic growths fingered their way upwards here, not yet joined with their fellow stalactites but straining upwards towards them with a few inches in between, so that they formed an arcade along the rim, like one of those fancy shelters built on the viewpoints overhanging famous water-falls. The lamp showed all this corner of the hall beautifully, while the ladder was now lost in absolute darkness at some distance from me, and I hoped and believed that someone was already half-way down it, and descending fast. From the top he wouldn't be able to see what I was up to at this end of the hall, he had no option but to descend, if he wanted to know, and he hadn't come all this way to turn back now.

The noise was splendid, and after a while rather terrible in its weight and monotony and force. It swallowed every other sound completely ; a whole platoon could have swung their way down the ladder, and I doubt if I should have heard anything. I took my time about what I had to do, taking care to stay where the lamp would shed its light full on me. I unwound my coil of cord, and attached one end of it to the handle of the brief-case, and then wound the other end about the foot of one of the stalagmites on the extreme edge of the drop, and made it fast there. Then I lowered the case carefully over the edge, and paid out the rope gently until it hung at full length. Not a place to leave valuables for any length of time, of course, but extremely safe and secret for the duration of an emergency, and virtually invisible even when you stood beside it, the brown cord against the soap-brown stone.

When it was done I sighed, and stretched, and even went

so far as to get out a cigarette and light it. Credible, I hoped, after the job was finished. Was he down yet ? Yes, surely ! But as for where, how near to me, how far from me, in which direction, I didn't yet know. It would be easier to hear when I walked back towards the ladder, away from the bellowing void, where the fine, drifting spray boiled up and filled the gulf like mist, and rose steaming between the glistening pillars of rock. I judged he must have seen enough during my descent to make now for the safe wall, where the curtain-like formations offered him cover. I strained my ears in that direction as I sauntered back towards the ladder. There'd been nothing to make him nervous. The ladders were fixed, he wouldn't suspect me of any intention of drawing them up after me. I checked over the dispositions, and couldn't see what should be able to go wrong.

I stubbed out my cigarette, and walked back steadily, and when the dangling ladder came into sight against the shiny brown wall I put out the lamp I carried, and went on with only the light from my helmet. But before I touched the ladder I had one hand on the switch of the strong light on my belt, and the other on the little gun in my pocket.

I passed not far from him. I don't know how I knew, whether it was really a slight sound I caught, or whether, as I imagined, the penetrating cold was suddenly softened by some infinitely slight but perceptible wave of human warmth. At least I had no doubts at the time, and I wasn't at fault. I orientated myself to him as to the pole, clinging to the magnetic point until my arm brushed the ladder. And just at that moment there was certainly a sound, curiously jarring because it shouldn't have come yet, it shouldn't have been necessary : a shifting, almost a scuffle in the darkness, at the point on which my whole being was centred, and an indrawn breath, sharp, brief, suddenly cut off into smothering silence.

I swung upon the sound with the full beam of the lamp,
the gun advanced in my hand.   The shaft of brilliance
sprang across the cave, snatching substance out of the darkness, building lofty, glistening walls of rock, casting abrupt
shadows.

" Stand where you are !   Don't move ! "

They didn't move. Crispin's eyes, enormous, desperate,
wild with fury and shame, stared at me mutely over the
coat-sleeve that was clamped round his shoulder and across
his face, half suffocating him, half lifting him from his feet.
His hands, raised to claw the arm away, hung arrested on
the air, his body, hoisted on to tiptoe, arched backwards in
a painfully distorted bow which rendered almost visible
the gun that was boring a hole in his back.

Clean over his head, and with several inches to spare at
that, the man who held him stared levelly at me, steadily
overlooking the dazzle of the lamp with narrowed, intent
eyes the colour of pack-ice, beneath a cliff-like forehead.
He wasn't Dermot, he wasn't David, he wasn't the stranger
in the garden who turned out to be no stranger.   Lean,
long cheeks drew down into a handsome, clear-cut jaw, a
short grey moustache lent a sub-military air to what might
otherwise have been a scholar's long, mobile, incisive
mouth.   Grizzled hair paled almost to white at the temples.
He must have been somewhere in the late fifties, at a guess.
If he resembled anybody in the case it was, in a broad,
generic way, Bruce Almond.

I knew him at once, though properly speaking I'd never
seen his face before except on the cover of a book.   He was
the factor we'd overlooked, the expert, the invisible man.
He was Professor John Barclay.

CHAPTER XIV

THERE WAS a long moment, as absurd as it was horrible, while we all stared and said nothing, while Crispin choked, and I made frantic reassessments and hectic guesses, and Barclay calculated and measured, and dropped his encircling arms quickly from the boy's mouth to clamp it cripplingly round both his arms just above the elbows. Crushed white, Crispin's cheeks slowly flushed as the blood flowed back into them, and the marks of the tweed sleeve reddened in his flesh like scars. He didn't say anything. He just looked at me with sick, angry, helpless eyes, very much as I must have been looking at him. And there was nothing to be said about it, and nothing to be done. I didn't dare to move so much as a muscle. It wasn't I who would have paid for it. Not first, at any rate.

Barclay smiled. When the long lips lengthened still more they looked thin and grey, and quite unamused. All the smile marked was a brief, nervous motion of satisfaction at the transfer of the initiative into his hands.

"Stand still!" he ordered me in his turn, in a clipped, brittle voice. "Don't try to be clever, don't switch off that light, don't move your hands. At the first move out of turn I shall make sure of the boy."

I believed him. I doubt if I've ever stood so still in my life.

The smile lengthened again into a grimace. "Yes," he said, "I thought he might come in useful, as soon as I felt him treading on my heels. That's why I took good care not to alarm him too soon. It was obliging of him to join the procession, wasn't it? If he hadn't, we should have been man to man and gun to gun—and on your home ground. I'm lucky ! "

I said nothing, and I didn't move. If he talked enough, he might even drop a crumb of an idea into my mind. God knows I needed one, I was blank enough at that moment.

" I'm afraid it's been a shock to you," he said civilly. " I'm sorry ! " He wasn't sorry. For the first time he did look almost amused.

" You're hurting him," I said, seeing Crispin's lip caught in his teeth. " Relax ! If you've got a gun in his back, what more do you want ? "

He took no notice of that, and he didn't slacken the tight grip of his arm that was dragging Crispin back on the gun. " And now," he said, as if I hadn't spoken, " would you mind walking to the near edge of that pothole, and tossing your gun into it ? Strictly for the boy's sake, of course. First put down that lantern, and leave it switched on. Good ! Now the gun, please. I shall see every move, so for his sake, control your reflexes. Just throw in the gun."

There was nothing I could do but obey, and with such ostentatious and deliberate movements that he should be in no doubt of my obedience. The searchlight beam from my waist moved from the two locked figures, proceeded before me across the hall to the glossy lip of the chasm. Spray smoked upwards gently in the concentration of light. The little pistol dropped out of sight like a shiny stone. In the chaos of ceaseless sound there wasn't an instant of impact, only a vanishing. The pit might have been bottomless.

" Good ! " said the voice behind me. " And now haul up that brief-case you've just lowered down there."

I took my time over it, but I also took good care to move so that he could see my hands throughout. I couldn't take any chances with Crispin's life, and there was that in the eyes, the voice, the set of the trap of a mouth, that made it clear this man wouldn't hesitate to kill. This seemed to me the furious, obsessed calm of one who had already a dead lamb behind him, and to whom a whole flock of sheep would be a small matter now in pursuit of the same end.

There was only one hope, and that was that he had somehow sold himself completely on the genuineness of my nocturnal mission, and would take the brief-case, locked and keyless as it was, and go away confident that he had what he'd come for. And leave us alive here, after we'd seen his face ? It was possible, if no better than possible. Nobody was ever going to prove anything in Bruce's case, so he didn't face a murder charge yet, and might still prefer to avoid killing, other things being equal ; all the more as he might well reason that we should be reluctant to bring the police into a case like this, which already concerned stolen property. A private war suited us better, as well as him. He'd kill coolly enough if he had to. But not if there was no extra dividend in it for him.

Then I stole a look sideways at his face as I hauled up the cord, the brief-case bumping against rock on its way up out of the dark ; and I couldn't be sure what he'd do. I knew nothing about him but the face, and that was the most uncomforting face I'd ever set eyes on, the most ferocious, and at the same time the most indifferent.

Glistening like a fish with fine spray, the brief-case lay at my feet again.

" Untie it from the stalagmite. Carry it to the foot of the ladder, and leave it there, with the cord. You won't, I hope, be so foolish as to go near enough to touch the ladder itself, will you ? "

I wasn't. I put the case where he told me to put it, and stood clear. When I faced them again, the beam of my lamp showed me Crispin's head lolling against the man's shoulder, and his eyes closed. His brows were drawn together in a painful, ruled line, his teeth were locked in his lower lip. If he hadn't been strung so taut I should have thought he'd fainted. He still hadn't uttered a sound.

"Now walk to the far end of the gallery. No tricks, or the boy here will be the first to suffer the consequences."

I went. What else could I do? But I went slowly, watching them every step of the way. They were still motionless against the rock wall, almost midway between me and the distant end of the hall, where I'd been told to go. As I drew almost level with them, Barclay said suddenly: "The case is locked?"

"You'll find out," I said, halting.

He ground the gun into Crispin's spine with a sudden vicious jab, and repeated in the same tone: "The case is locked?"

"Yes," I said, sweating with a rage so sudden that I could hardly keep my face and my voice steady.

"Where's the key? Have you got it?"

"Not here. It's in my room at the Lawns."

He seemed to believe it. He said with a shrug: "Go on. To the far end." After all, a lock wouldn't delay him long. I took two more steps, slowly, reluctant to pass them and move on out of reach. Would he, by any lucky chance, open the case here? No, I threw that idea out at once. He'd be a fool to deflect his attention even for a moment from the two of us, and he wasn't a fool. No, even if he already suspected that it was a fake, he'd take it up with him to the upper gallery to examine it at leisure. There was no way out of here for us except by that rope ladder, and that route he controlled from the top so long as he held the gun. So why should he take risks, and why should he hurry? No, there wasn't going to be any heaven-sent moment of greed or impatience in which he'd take his eyes off me long enough for me to take action. I gave up the idea.

I was abreast of them when Crispin suddenly sagged

downwards with his whole weight, collapsing limply into the arm that held him, and flowing through it to the ground. I saw the faint begin, if you can talk of the beginning of something that was all over and done in an instant, and I knew it wasn't a faint, and I saw it being a death before he reached the floor. I yelled : " No, Crispin, *no* ! You damned fool ! " and leaped towards them, at least to deflect the inevitable reprisals if I could, at best maybe to take the moment he'd tried to offer me.

His collapse was so unexpected that it almost came off. He slid through the circling arm like quicksilver, and flowed from before the barrel of the gun. And as he dropped he reached up and gripped Barclay's gun-wrist, and dragged down on it over his shoulder with all his might, arching his back violently against his enemy's shins.

The gun went off, the sound of the shot reverberating round and round furiously from wall to wall. Then I was on the rock floor, rolling helplessly, trying to draw up my knees and climb to my feet again, trying to reach Crispin, and crumpling back to the ground at every heave. I felt the blood streaming out of my thigh before I felt the pain. Curious, pulsating moments of faintness passed over me, and in between them I saw, with peculiar, acid clarity, the end of Crispin's bid for victory.

If only he'd had a bit more muscle he might have hauled his enemy clean off-balance over his crouching body, and laid him out cold against the rock. But he hadn't the weight to go with his courage, and I'd known it from the start. Braced back on long, firm legs, Barclay withstood the pull, and in the first instant when it relaxed he took Crispin by the hair with his left hand, and yanked him viciously to his feet. A knee was driven hard into the small of his back. He shot several yards towards the narrowing end of the gallery, and fell on his face with a dull, heavy, gasping fall, horribly winded.

I was on one knee, the right, the only one that would work, and I saw, heard, felt that fall as though it had happened to my own body. I lunged at a large foot that seemed for a moment almost within my reach, but it was yards from me. I felt the blood going out of me more rapidly, and then the pain ran through my thigh like fire, and I passed out.

I came round once, vaguely and only for an instant, to a nightmarish awareness of the great flood of light pouring along the rock floor from my body, as though I bled light, and Crispin there in the pallid pool, some little distance from me, heaving and gasping and drawing great painful gulps of air, as though he were drowning in my pale, shed blood. He was crouched doubled-up over his folded arms, fighting for breath, his face hidden from me. I wanted to get to him, but when I tried to drag myself along I went down again into the dark.

CHAPTER XV

WHEN I CAME round for the second time Crispin was kneeling over me, and there was a knot of hard, congested pain eating through my groin, and a great deal of light all round us both, no longer proceeding out of my body, but beaming upwards from the floor of the cave beside me. He'd taken off my belt, and set to work on stopping the bleeding. His face hung over me, hollow and brilliant with highlights and deep shadows, like a Rembrandt. He looked sick, but composed. Dirty, too, and grazed all down one cheek, and his breath still wheezed a bit. He must have dragged himself across to me as soon as he could crawl.

He saw me open my eyes, and stopped twisting the pencil, or whatever it was he was using to tighten the knotted handkerchief round my groin. He smiled at me. It was an effort, but he did it.

" I know there's no way of getting a really effective tourniquet on the femoral," he said apologetically, " but I'm expecting to need my thumbs."

They were the oddest words anybody could possibly have produced in the circumstances, but they were pure Crispin. I found myself thinking, in an irresponsible way, that living up to him was going to be a problem. If, of course, we lived.

" Where is he ? " I asked.

" Just disappeared in the top gallery. He took the other lamp. Even with you crippled he wasn't taking any chances on examining his catch down here. Why should he ? He's got plenty of time. I took all the change out of your trouser pocket," said Crispin, " to knot inside my handkerchief for a pressure pad. I hope you don't mind. Afraid it's horribly uncomfortable, but I couldn't think of anything else."

In less than five minutes he'd done everything that could be done for me. I felt downwards laboriously at my thigh, with a hand that seemed to weigh like lead. Below the drawn cord of linen cutting into my groin the trouser leg was slit away, and there was a thick, soft bandage knotted tightly round the wound.

" What did you use ? "

" My singlet, there wasn't anything else. I'm not cold," he said defensively, his chin wobbling for a moment.

He shouldn't have said the word. I'd been too deep in my stupor to realise until then how the cold bit down here. There was a lot of moisture round me on the stone, and it wasn't water ; it clung to my fingers, and under my leg it was still hot from the wound.

" Artery ? Are you sure ? "

He nodded miserably. " Not the main one, I think, or I couldn't have stopped it. The tourniquet seems to be holding it fairly well. Only you can't risk keeping it on too long."

"I'm all right," I said. You couldn't even consider it as a lie, since it had no intention and no hope of deceiving him about anything. He sat back on his heels, and pushed the tangled hair back from his forehead, and we looked at each other, and knew we were as good as done for, knew it wouldn't be long before the man above came back to ask us the question only Crispin could answer. He had the means of persuasion, in case we were obstinate. And it was I who had picked this place, of all places, for the showdown between us, and drawn the boy here after me.

"I'm sorry, Cris," I said. "I made an infernal mess of it."

"You didn't. It was my fault. It's my fault you're hurt, and if—if we—that will be my fault, too. If I hadn't followed you it would have been man to man and gun to gun, just as he said. That was what you intended, wasn't it?"

"Why the hell," I said feebly, "couldn't you have gone on sleeping, and stayed out of this?"

"I wasn't asleep. I felt your hand under the pillow, and I knew you'd taken the gun. I got up and listened at your door, and you were moving about in there, and I dressed, just to be ready, in case anything happened. When you went down the stairs I followed you."

"Where did I pick him up? In the garden?"

"Yes. I saw him come out of the shrubbery and slip through the gate after you. I thought I was making a good job of trailing you both, without either of you knowing I was there. I thought I could be useful." The most rueful of smiles hollowed his grazed cheek for a moment, and vanished. "And this is what I've done to you!"

"Don't be a fool! How could you have known what I was trying to do? The only justification I could possibly have had," I said wryly, "for taking the affair out of your hands was if I could make the better job of it. Including hoodwinking you. It seems I couldn't even do that properly. You were supposed to be fast asleep in your bed while we settled the account. I should have known! When the key wasn't in the lock, that should have been enough for me."

"I knew why you locked me in," said Crispin quickly. "I didn't blame you, only I couldn't let you do it again. It wasn't because I didn't trust you that I followed you. I knew you were on my side, but—— You do see, don't you, that I had to know what you were doing? It was my affair, I couldn't just lie there and let it be taken from me, like that."

"No," I said, feeling the prickly pains of cramp beginning to gnaw at my leg, "you couldn't do that. I was as presumptuous as all the rest. I couldn't allow you to run your own feud your own way. I had to take it out of your hands. And all I've done is wreck it."

"It was a wreck already," said Crispin.

A wave of pain and nausea rolled over me, and the light went dark again, but only for a few strange seconds. Then the boy was again beside me, bending over me anxiously, whispering: "Evelyn!"

"All right, Cris, I'm all right! Crispin—I can't turn my head far enough to look—is there any sign of him near the top of the ladder?—any light? Could you get up there unnoticed? There's plenty of cover there, you could slip out when he comes down again. If we put out this light he won't see from above that he's lost one of us."

He didn't even look, he didn't clutch at the words or the idea. He just smiled his wry, unchildish smile at me, and shook his head. "He looped up the end of the ladder and pulled it up after him to the first stage. There's no going up that way until somebody's climbed down and released it. He didn't forget anything. He doesn't forget things."

He was leaning very close to me. I remember the beads

of drying blood along his scratches, and the distortion of his already swollen cheek, and his eyes, large and awed and wild, shining distressfully on me.

" And I never thought of him ! " he said bitterly. " Who was more likely to know what value to set on a find like that ? And who knew better than he did that Bruce would accept whatever he said about it without a murmur ? And it was too simple ! I never even thought of him ! " He passed a hand over his soiled forehead, and knuckled wearily at his eyes. I could feel him trembling suddenly against my flank with bitterness and rage, damning himself for his shortsightedness. It wasn't at the dig, it wasn't on the journey to Athens in David's care, that Crispin's mask had vanished, and left a fake in its place. It was in Barclay's office in Athens. He must have needed only one look at the thing, and a moment's consideration of the as yet un-tapped tomb from which it came, to realise that this was one of the most fabulous finds since Schliemann. And even experts, even respected authorities, it seems, retain enough humanity to covet another man's discovery ; especially, perhaps, if luck has dropped the prize into a slapdash, undeserving hand like Bruce Almond's.

Was it the gold he wanted ? Or the kudos ? Whatever it was, there was an easy way for him to get it. Keep the mask, copy it, send back the fake—he could hardly write and say the thing was worthless without returning it, experts don't simply make away with the specimens, however bogus, referred to them for an opinion. But who was better placed to provide the substitute than he was, with all the varied good and bad relics at his disposal ?

" It was long odds against anyone taking the trouble to examine the thing closely, after *he* returned it," went on Crispin, worrying at his wounds. " In any case, he sent it back one post later than his letter to Bruce, so that nobody could take a look at it immediately. By the time it arrived the row was over, and everybody wanted the whole thing forgotten. Bruce didn't even open the parcel. And that same night he was killed. After that, who was even going to remember a silly little affair like our bad joke ? Nobody ! "

" But Barclay was in Athens," I objected.

" You can get from Athens to Pirithoön in a few hours by car. Nobody ever inquired into Professor Barclay's movements. Why should they ? He could be anywhere he pleased. All he had to do was drive there by the track on the other side of the acropolis, get hold of Bruce alone, and get him to go up to the citadel with him, and just put a bullet or a knife in his back. He could be back in Athens long before morning."

He was right, he had to be right. And it had all gone according to plan, except that when the murderer went to gloat over his gains he found the tomb rifled and the gold gone, and a signed invitation left for him by the side of the dead. An invitation he had accepted.

I was drifting down into the dark again, and into an icy coldness. I felt Crispin's hand at my thigh, and heard his indrawn breath of dismay. " It's coming through the padding. And I haven't got anything else I can use ! "

I wondered if it mattered. I was a long way down, and coming back was a lot of trouble, but there was something bothering me still, something that could be done, if only I could remember what it was. Injured men die of exposure rather easily in caves ; even a slight injury can write you off down there, once it prevents you from moving. But Crispin could move. Crispin could go, if only there was a way out without using the ladder. Not that he would, of course, if he realised what I was booked for, but I could tell him to go and fetch help for me, and maybe he wasn't experienced enough to know how little use it would be by the time it arrived.

My mind was rocking in a cradle of icy cold, a long way

down in a well of darkness; and two eyes were staring down the well at me, great, wild eyes above a moving mouth that shouted entreaties I couldn't hear. I saw him as you see someone in one of those convex mirrors, distant, tiny but clear. He was feeling with his palms at my cheeks, at my forehead and hands. He was tugging at the zipper of his wind-jacket, peeling it off, wriggling out of his sweater——

I put up my hands and caught him by the arms, and the movement shook me loose from my bed of ice, and sent me plunging up the long shaft of darkness into the bright light of the lamp, and the piercing reality of my situation and his, and I knew as I touched him, and felt how slight he was between my palms, what it was that could still be done. By him, not by me.

I held and shook him, pulling down his arms. " Put that on again ! Put it on ! Do as I tell you ! "

" No, I'm all right ! You have the sweater, I don't need it, I can move, and you can't. Evelyn, you must—you're icy cold ! "

I pulled the sweater down brusquely, like dressing an obstinate child. We'd lost too much time already. " Put on your wind-jacket, you're going to need it. You're getting out of here. I can't, but you can, and you're going to. That tunnel from the end of the gallery there, the one we tried, the one that got too tight for me—— There was fresh air coming through that tunnel from somewhere beyond. There must be a way through there. Here, take the helmet, you'll need it. Get out if you can find a way safely, but don't take any risks. Do you hear me ? If it gets too small for you, or if you get through into another gallery but can't find a way out, lie up and wait. He won't stay long here when he knows there's nothing for him. He daren't. And he wouldn't be able to get to you, even if he knew where you were. If I can't pass there, he can't. Don't come out this way again until he's gone." I pushed the helmet towards him, and he didn't move, didn't touch it. "What are you waiting for? Get on with it! Go on!"

"I can't!" he said, trembling. "I'm not going to leave you here." His voice was low and hurried, but steadier than the rest of him. He'd achieved a kind of balance of despair, and I was trying to push him off it into the vertigo of hope. And he knew better than to believe in it, but the push had upset him just the same.

"If you don't leave me we're both of us done for. You're mobile, I'm not, you're small enough to go where I can't. My only chance is for you to get out alive and bring help. You must see that. So go, quickly, before he comes back. It can't be long now."

"No!" he said. "I couldn't possibly get anyone in time, and you know it. He's taken his time, but you're right, it can't be long now. Not half long enough! Even if I'd gone immediately, it wouldn't have been long enough. If you can't get away, I can't, either. How could I? He'll be back to ask where the gold is. And he won't know that you really don't know, and if you tell him so he won't believe you. So I can't leave you, can I?"

"I can tell him where it is," I persisted, dragging myself up on my elbow, feeling the tourniquet shift, and the blood pulse hot through Crispin's saturated singlet. "I can tell him a dozen safe places clear of these caves, send him miles away."

"He won't believe you! If he does, he still won't let you get out of here until he's tested what you tell him. You don't believe he's such a fool! Evelyn, *please*, you're making it bleed worse——"

"I can hold out long enough for you to get away," I said, shaking him furiously, and hurting myself abominably with every motion. "Do as I tell you! Go! *Now!*"

"No!" He tried to put his arms round me and hold me still, but I thrust him off. "You'd be dead before I could get back, if I left you with him. We can't afford to lie! Not even to stall! Evelyn, don't! Don't make me!"

"Are you going?" I laid hold of his careful tourniquet, and twisted it, and felt the surge and scalding heat of blood. He gave a little, helpless, angry cry, and tried to pull my hand away. "If you don't, I'll pull it off. Do you hear?"

"No, I can't! You mustn't! *Please!* Oh, my God!" he said in a whimper, through chattering teeth, "what am I to do?"

"Are you going?" He hesitated still, and I felt myself beginning to sink again into the first waves of the encroaching darkness about which he must know nothing. There was no time to argue with him. I heaved myself up wildly, and hit him clumsily and weakly on his unbruised cheek; and suddenly he jerked away with a sob, and snatched up the helmet.

"All right, I'm going! Tighten it again! I will go, I'll do whatever you say!" He hung over me in agonised distrust for an instant, and then he gave up the struggle and ran wildly towards the dark, distant corner where the tunnel was hidden. I remember hearing how abruptly his footsteps faded, but whether because he ran so fast or because I sank so fast I couldn't tell. As though he'd released the only hold that was sustaining me on the surface of consciousness, down I went in a long plunge, like a stone. I'd got rid of him just in time, only just in time. Now I could sink, and stay down.

CHAPTER XVI

SOMETHING was fluttering against my cheek, a moist, soft touch like a butterfly's wing. Something was heavy and clinging across my body, and there was a curious, comforting pressure all down my left side. Not hard and cold like rock, but warm and firm, and not quite still, as things alive are never quite still. I think I was aware of my gratitude for it before I was aware of the contact itself. I lay still, and all the energy I had yet regained was devoted to being thankful for it. Then I moved my hand a little, to find out what it was that lay so gently over me, and rubbed between my fingers the soft, thick texture of wool. I could reach only to my waist under this mysterious covering, and then there was something heavy and warm that embraced me above it, holding me closely. And this girdling warmth, most strangely, felt my questing touch beneath it, and lifted from me a little of its weight. I disentangled my arm slowly, with infinite effort, felt down my right side until I encountered another hand, and then followed wonderingly across my own body by way of a slender arm, very thinly clad in the sleeve of a gaberdine wind-jacket and apparently nothing else, an arched, protective shoulder lying over my left shoulder and chest, to a smooth chin, a cold cheek, short, curling hair, a familiar head pressed into the hollow of my neck, the forehead against my cheek. He hadn't gone. He wasn't safe on the other side of the tunnel of rock, but here lying beside me, breathing into my throat, giving me the only thing he had left to give me, his warmth to keep me alive.

" Crispin——"

" I couldn't get through," he whispered, " it wasn't big enough. I was frightened to go on. I did try, Evelyn." He had it all ready to pour into my ear the moment I came round, too quickly, too anxiously. He wasn't a good liar, even when his heart was in it.

" Am I hurting you ? Am I too heavy ? "

" No. Your sweater—put it on ! Don't be a fool ! "

He didn't move, except to spread it more carefully over me.

" How do you feel now ? A bit warmer ? "

" Much warmer," I said, lying, too. My voice, with all the volume I could give it, sounded infinitely distant. He was shivering so that only his steady contact with me through the whole length of his body helped him to control the convulsions. And I couldn't even make him take notice of me and save himself. If there'd been a hundred ways out, he wouldn't have taken one of them unless he could have carried me along with him.

" Evelyn," he whispered, " in case we don't get out of here intact—I'm sorry ! And thanks ! "

" Thanks for what ? For leading you into this trap ? "

" Just thanks ! " he repeated obstinately.

" Crispin—in case we *do*—— "

" Yes ? " He quaked at the very suggestion, ready to hope even against reason.

" I'll have the hide off you for being such a pigheaded little fool."

A gusty little laugh blew down my neck, and thawed my congealing flesh. He tightened his arm over me in what at first I took to be a reflex spasm from cold or cramp, not supposing that he could be offering me something so simple and elemental as a hug. His cheek quivered against mine, and I felt his lashes fluttering wildly, leaving on my face a light, hot dew of tears. And in the same moment a flickering light swung and swung again over the upper reaches of the rocks above my eyes, and Crispin stiffened into strained attention beside me.

" He's on the ladder. He's coming down."

The best moment of my life, and it had to be almost the last !

CHAPTER XVII

CRISPIN PUSHED me gently back as he got slowly to his feet, and disengaged himself just as gently from my cold hands when I tried to retain my hold on him. By the time I had managed to inch myself a yard or so after him on my right side, scrabbling with toe and hip and elbow, he was half-way across to the foot of the ladder, going to meet his enemy. What followed I saw in a series of nightmares, each a few moments long, each a little larger and louder than the last, as I crawled towards them like a trampled snail. Between the nightmares I suppose I either fainted, or at least sank just below the level of consciousness necessary to seeing and hearing. As for pain, I can't remember much of it. My left leg dragged after me like a dead log, with no feeling left in it, leaving new smears on the russet stone.

Crispin walked forward steadily, smoothing back his dis-ordered hair, and brushing down his soiled, wet jacket with his palms, as though he wanted to tidy himself up for an interview of the greatest importance. His face I couldn't see, but there was no need ; I knew every line and every expression of it by heart.

I saw the bobbing light that was slung at Barclay's waist step sidewise to the ground at the foot of the ladder, and turn in an arc of reddish, yellowish colours round a seg-ment of the wall, to leap like a lance across the cave towards us. It met and mingled with the greater light beaming upwards from our lamp, and the advancing figure behind took shape, tall, long-armed, long-legged, large and light of movement like an athlete. I saw the big, broad, lofty brow like a plane of worked stone, and the eyes beneath it might have been inlaid with mother-of-pearl and lapis lazuli, like the bright, opaque, acquisitive eyes of the stone figures of Egyptian scribes. A handsome, authoritative man with a dry, scholarly accent, a hungrily resolute manner, and a levelled gun in his hand. He showed no change of face at having been taken in once ; it was no more than he had expected, and he didn't grudge the time spent in checking a lead which had proved to be false. He was too much a scientist to try to economise in effort at the expense of efficiency.

" Where is the gold ? " he asked, in the same precise, impersonal voice we'd first heard from him, and the gun hitched upwards by a few suggestive degrees, and pointed thoughtfully at Crispin's chest.

" You're wasting your time asking him," I said, resting on my elbow to have enough energy for speech, since it seemed I couldn't hope to do two things at once. " He gave it to me to keep for him. He doesn't know what I've done with it."

My voice sounded loud to me, louder than theirs, but they didn't seem to hear it. They were too intent on each other to remember or be aware of anyone else. They stood almost within touch of each other, Crispin drawn up tall and slender and rigid with hate. He'd lost touch with fear, there was no room in him for fear when he stood face to face with the man who had killed Bruce, any more than hounds crossing a road on a hot scent can pause to be afraid of the car that runs them down, or stop hunting merely because they're maimed after it has passed.

" How did you kill my father ? " asked Crispin, in the direct, purposeful, interested voice of one opening an academic inquiry. " Was he still in the office that night, alone, when you came up to the dig ? "

The gun pricked up and levelled gently in the pale, well-tended hand, stretching its muzzle hopefully towards the boy. He didn't seem to see it.

" Where is the gold ? " The question this time had the first ominous hint of impatience in it. When Professor Barclay lectured he must have been able to cause ill-prepared students to liquefy inwardly with that tone.

" You're wasting your time," I repeated. " I'm the only one who knows that. Send him away, and I'll tell you."

" Did you go to him and say you were worried about your snap judgment ? " pursued Crispin. " Did you suggest having a look at the site of the find ? Is that how you got him out there alone with you, where it would be easy to put a bullet in him when his back was turned ? I expect you found it easier with the victim's back turned, the first time. I see you're getting more confidence now."

The gun didn't waver, but Barclay's left hand rose out of the shadow, and struck the boy in the face with the full weight of a long arm behind it, once, and a back-handed flick in returning, and again, and again. Crispin stood like a tree, received the blows with no more movement than they enforced on him, and straightened his head instantly to resume his insatiable pursuit.

" *Where is the gold ?* "

" You won't get anything out of him like that," I croaked, swallowing nausea and rage and tears of helplessness, and grating my broken nails into the rock that slid moistly under me. " Even if he knew he wouldn't tell you. But he doesn't know. Send him home, and I'll tell you where to find your damned gold."

" Send him home ! " Barclay repeated it with a thin smile, without taking his eyes from the boy's face for an instant. " So that he can bring the police down on us ? "

"Don't be a fool! How can he go to the police? He stole the stuff, and you know it. A word to the police, and he's in bad trouble himself, as bad as yours."

"I don't think," said the thin, mobile lips thoughtfully, "that that would deter him, if he could salvage you. I'm quite sure it wouldn't, if he could destroy me."

Crispin drew a steadying breath, and resumed in the same detached, inquiring tone, as though he had neither heard nor felt anything since he himself last spoke: "Which were you going to be, gold-rich or fame-rich, Professor Barclay? Money's nice, but it would have to be only a private enjoyment, wouldn't it? It's difficult to dispose of such exceptional pieces, and then, you'd be losing the specialist's pleasure in them. In any case, the find would have made headlines worth a lot of money, wouldn't it? Not to mention what you could make writing books about how you found my father's discovery. My father's tomb! You made sure it should be that, didn't you?"

Quite coldly, taking care that the boy saw it coming, well assured that he would not move an inch to evade it, Barclay swung a deliberate fist, and knocked him down. It was done with precision and ferocity. I heard the crunch of his knuckles into Crispin's cheek and jaw, and somehow I was a yard nearer to the enemy, and all the life I had left in me was thrusting me nearer with clawing fingers, lugging my dead log after me as best I could.

First I was boring through a red fog, and then through a black, and when next I got my eyes clear, and swallowed the choking gall that filled my mouth, Crispin was just lifting himself from the ground. He sat for a few minutes leaning on one arm, his head hanging, his hand pressed to his face. He never made a sound, simply sat there containing the pain and stupor until he should be able to master them, and return to the hunt. The blow had flung him several yards aside from his position between Barclay and me, and Barclay had made a half-turn where he stood, in order to continue facing the boy. Only his shoulder was now turned towards me, and in any case, he'd written me off. Crispin shook his head slowly back and forth, and under his tangled hair his eyes flashed one live, calculating glance at me. Then he pushed himself up from the ground, and lurched to his feet.

I thought he was going to collapse again. He seemed too dazed to be able to orientate himself, why else should he turn his back on his enemy, and stagger several steps in the wrong direction? Barclay followed his movements carefully, revolving on one heel. His back was turned on me now. I was so far gone in fury and weakness and shock that it took me a full minute to realise that that was what Crispin had intended. Only a few yards separated me from the long legs and well-shod feet that were all I could see clearly of Bruce's murderer. Crispin never stopped fighting, not even when he was half stunned.

I gathered what strength I had left, and heaved myself nearer, and the floor heaved with me and curled up over me like a breaking sea. Through the momentary darkness, muffled and distant, I heard the insistent, famished voice demanding with a sharper inflection : " Where is the gold ? I advise you to answer me now rather than later."

" If we go on long enough," gasped Crispin from between his steadying hands, still shaking his head numbly to and fro, " I shan't be able to answer. But what will that get you ? "

I stretched out my right arm, and my finger-tips brushed helplessly at the floor six inches from the heel of Barclay's right shoe. If I could pluck him round to the right as he fell, even if the gun went off, the shot, with a grain of luck, should fly wide. I sprawled on my face on the lurching stone sea, and strained forward again, and at that moment Crispin, afraid, I think, to let the thread of words and movement slacken for an instant for fear his enemy's attention should again remember me, lowered his hands and took one short, deliberate step forward.

It was the bravest, the craziest, the most terrifying thing I ever saw, and heaven knows it deserved to succeed ; and it did move Barclay a corresponding step backwards, the gun pricking up like an angry little snake in his hand. But instead of giving ground directly in order to keep his distance, he suddenly sprang aside, in that very moment recollecting me. My fingers plucked at the tweed of his trouser leg, but failed to get a hold, and before I could lunge again he had lifted his foot and stamped it down upon my hand, grinding my fingers into the rock with a frenzied twist of his heel. Sickening pain surged along my arm and burst in my face like an explosive charge, and Crispin gave an angry, hurt cry, as if for the first time he, too, was aware of pain.

It was more than enough to betray him. Barclay withdrew his foot from my broken hand, and stepped back a wary pace or two to keep both of·us in view ; and the gun turned from Crispin, and lowered its squat muzzle to explore me.

" We'll waste no more time. You have one minute to tell me what you've done with the gold, or he has one minute to live. If you lie, that won't save him. No one except myself knows you're here, and you'll stay here, both of you, until I have that gold in my hands. Time is of importance for your friend. Look at him ! "

Crispin was looking at me indeed, and trembling.

" Two more hours down here will certainly kill him," said Barclay, considering me with his cold, appraising eyes. " It's up to you. Kill him immediately, if you think it worth it, or slowly, if you think you can outwit me. Or hand over the gold to me, and keep him in exchange. Well ? Your minute begins *now* ! "

Crispin closed his eyes for an instant to say farewell to all the vows he'd made to Bruce's indignant ghost, and couldn't keep, swallowed hard, and opened them again to look down at me with a pale, heroic smile. He didn't hesitate, and he didn't lie.

"The gold's here," he said, "not ten yards from where the decoy was. I haven't got the key here, but I give you my word this time it really is the gold."

"Bring it to me."

Crispin turned and walked to the rim of the gulf, and passed out of my sight. I couldn't raise myself any longer to look after him, my trampled hand had no power, and even drawing it along the ground towards my body transfixed it so instantaneously with knives and needles of pain that I knew several small bones were broken in it. I'd got my tanning as my share of the results of Dorothy's wonderful idea, all right, but it was nothing to what Crispin was suffering at that moment, and I knew it. And there was nothing I could do to help him. Even if my life hadn't been there to bargain with, it would only have meant that Crispin himself would be tormented until he gave in. So there was no point even in dying.

He came back slowly, first his shadow across me from the lamp, then Crispin himself standing with his eyes turning anxious and large on me, and a big black despatch-box of japanned steel in his arms. "It was on a ledge just under the lip of the hole there," he said, and it was to me he was saying it. "I put it there last Thursday night, before Dermot came." He looked across me at Barclay. "Do you want me to give it to you? Or put it on the ground?"

"On the ground—here." I felt him give back a few steps towards the ladder; he was taking no chances, even with one tired and battered boy and a man half dead. "Now go back to your friend." The word sounded queer in his mouth. I wondered if he'd ever had any. Only colleagues, students, theories and academic distinctions, I should think.

The shot made me start and shudder; I hadn't been expecting it, and flung out my good hand to clutch at Crispin in terror that it had been fired point-blank at him. But he caught up my hand reassuringly between his own, and dropped to his knees on the rock beside me. " Not me," he said, with a tremor of angry laughter in his voice, " only the padlock ! I couldn't expect him to take my word for it, I suppose."

It was already a killing weight on what was left of my mind that we couldn't take his. Not that he'd promised us life, but it had been implied in the bargain ; and we couldn't rely on him to honour it, I realised that. Not after all we knew, not with the gold gone, and nothing left for us to lose and revenge to gain by drawing the police into the fight. I dreaded the moment when Crispin would grasp the truth, too, when the ladder would be drawn up and leave us buried alive, or the gun fired again, twice, to make sure that we should never talk about what we knew. At least with our tongues. What our bodies would be able to tell would hardly identify this highly-respected person who was scarcely known to either of us, and whose connection even with Crispin was so tenuous as to be practically non-existent.

" No silencer on this one," said Crispin, his lips curling with detestation. " Or was it a knife you used on Bruce ? "

No answer. It no longer mattered how he used his tongue, there was no longer any need to knock him down in order to demonstrate that insolence didn't pay. He was going to learn that lesson once and for all. Not that wisdom and compliance would have saved him.

I heard a deeply drawn breath of satisfaction and achievement that paid tribute to the treasure of Pirithoön, and even conveyed something of what it meant to the man

who had killed for it. Then the clash of the box closing.
He had what he'd come for. What would he do ? Shoot
us now, and pitch us into the underground river ? Or
simply draw up the ladder and leave us here ? No, not
that, he took no chances, and there was always the odd
chance that someone would come caving. He couldn't know
how very seldom that did happen. No, better for him if
we never turned up alive, but best of all if we never turned
up again even dead. He'd shoot us and drop us over into
the chasm. It didn't entirely preclude our bodies reappear-
ing some day, but it offered the best odds against it.

But I was wrong. With a sense of incredulity I heard his
voice saying : " You realise I could very well dispose of
you both with no risk to myself ? Supposing I propose a
bargain with you, instead. I'll leave you here alive, and with
the means of getting out, if you'll give me your word not
to move from here for just ten minutes after I'm gone, and
not to give information to the police. If you want your
revenge, come yourself and get it. After ten minutes you
can go and get help for your friend—if you do it on my
terms. If you prefer to see him die of exposure, that's up
to you."

I still didn't believe it. He hadn't found Crispin's word
good enough for him in the matter of the treasure, there
was something very wrong if he professed himself ready to
accept it now. I doubted if he ever took anyone's word for
anything. I tried to pluck Crispin back to me, but he was
on his feet in surprise and hope and doubt, staring at his
enemy, and the words were already leaping to his lips.
" All right, I promise ! "

And after all, what was the good of my speaking ? Whatever Barclay had in mind, we were in no position to cross
him. Yet he couldn't possibly mean what he said, why was
he saying it ? He really was walking backwards cautiously
towards the ladder, the despatch-box under his arm. He

kept his bleak, stone face turned towards us, and the gun ready in his hand, while he corded up the box at the foot of the climb, and tied the cord round his waist. The slack end of the ladder, which lay a yard or so along the floor of the cave, he belted in with the cord, too. Crispin observed it, and understood, and yet didn't understand.

" Thought you were taking my word for it ! " he said contemptuously. " You shall have your ten minutes, don't be afraid ! "

The unamused grey smile contorted the emotionless mouth. " The temptation might be too much for you," he said. " I've found you rather an impetuous young man."

Still Crispin didn't understand, but what was the use of pointing out to him the significance of what he himself had accidentally said ? Barclay *was* afraid ! Not afraid enough to draw back, once launched on this dangerous career, but afraid enough to suffer agonies of distrust and nervous tension with every inflexible step forward, afraid even of a battered boy and a half-dead man, if he should ever provide the least grain of a chance for them to astonish him. Even the gun could only make him feel safe so long as Crispin retained some hope to hold him back from extreme heroism. If he knew he was going to die in any case, he would launch himself at his enemy like an arrow, and who knew if the demon luck wouldn't tip the scale in his favour ? As Barclay had said, he was an impetuous young man. There was a lot of truth-telling going on down there under the earth.

No, this cautious man wasn't taking even the last, least chance with anyone who hated him as Crispin did. Before the boy realised that we'd both been condemned to death, Barclay was going to be out of his reach. Not, I thought, beating my labouring brain desperately, at the top of the oubliette, because his range of fire wouldn't be complete enough to cover the whole gallery from there. No, from somewhere on the ladder, above the fixed stage where the rock wall bulged again, where he could see every part of the gallery and yet be far out of our reach, that was the place he'd choose. True, the ladder might sway a little there, and interfere slightly with his aim, but he was undoubtedly used to handling a gun, and probably a good shot, and in any case he had, I reflected, four bullets at least to divide between us, and he'd need no more than one for a sitting target like me. As for lying to us in the meantime, to keep Crispin quiet, and making a bargain he had no intention of keeping, that was a purely practical move on his part. Afterwards he could simply climb down again, and tip us into the river without the slightest risk to himself.

I wondered how he'd ever ventured to come near enough to Crispin to hit him, even with the gun in the other hand. But of course, he'd learned a lot about Crispin since then. Especially that deliberate, defiant step forward, that had almost delivered his enemy to my clutching hand. No, he wasn't risking a Crispin without hope, and still within touch of him.

" Crispin," I called urgently, " come here ! "

Barclay's foot was on the ladder, he began to climb.

Crispin came with his chin on his shoulder, his eyes following the thin metal treads of the ladder as it began to curl upon itself and leave the ground. I reached up and caught at his sleeve, pulling him to his knees beside me.

" Just once do as I tell you, and don't argue. Go through that tunnel and get out of here. *At once* ! *Run* ! "

He stared at me with huge, tired eyes, and didn't move. Barclay was fifteen feet from the floor, and climbing at ease.

" Why ? He'll drop the ladder after he's got his start——"
As soon as he'd said it, he knew that he wouldn't. I saw his dirty cheeks blanch beneath the stains and bruises, and his lips part in realisation.

" Never mind why, *go* ! "

He didn't go. He stared at the blank wall that had sud-

denly and finally closed his world off from any future, and
he saw motives and actions resolve themselves into the
clarity they never have but side by side with the certainty
of death. I caught at his arm with my single hand, shaking
him feebly, imploring him to do what I asked, not to waste
his life, not to kill me twice over. He put his hand over
mine, and looked at me for a moment with a perverse, wild
smile, and shook his head. Then he began to laugh, not
hysterically, not out of bravado, but with an irresistible
shout of contemptuous, astonished amusement.

" So that was why——— Oh, *no* ! He was *frightened* ! "

" Crispin," I begged, groaning with impotence.

Barclay had reached his stragetic point, and was turning
at leisure to hook his left arm firmly in the ladder, and free
his right for our execution. He was in no hurry, he could
afford to take his time. He steadied the lamp at his waist,
adjusting the angle so that it lit us adequately.

" Frightened ! " cried Crispin, whirling round on his
knees to face the ladder, and stretching his body erect
between me and the gun. If I was a sitting target, he would
be one, too. If I couldn't run, and dodge, and hide from
the light, neither would he. He hugged to his body with one
exultant arm his own mysterious triumph, and the humiliation of his enemy.

" Of course ! Only somebody as timid and crafty as that
could have slipped a bullet in my father's back ! Well, this
one will have to be in front—if you have the nerve, Professor
Barclay ! Have you ? *Even from there* ? "

The light, reflected upwards from the sheen of the wet
rock, gleamed on the opaque eyes as on flat metal, with a
dead, malignant lustre, as Barclay raised his hand, and
slowly trained the pistol upon Crispin's breast.

CHAPTER XVIII

I REMEMBER STILL, in occasional nightmares, the moment of abnormal clarity in which distance and darkness seemed to be wiped out for me, and I saw the slow and methodical tightening of Barclay's finger on the trigger as intimately as though his braced hand had been only a yard from my eyes. There was nothing to be done about it, no means of argument, no tricks left to be played, nothing, and yet as long as there was the fraction of a fraction of an instant of life remaining I couldn't give up. I found a voice from somewhere, and the strength to throw up my one sound hand and point upwards at the small, dark bottle-neck of the oubliette above Barclay's head.

" Look ! Lights ! There's someone up there ! "

Crispin caught his breath and jerked up his head to stare where I pointed. There was one incalculable instant while Barclay himself was tempted. He was easily frightened, but not so easily deceived. He wavered for a breath, a tremor briefer than the passing of the light I hadn't seen. Then his finger continued the deliberate squeeze upon the trigger. And in the same instant a tongue of light, hardly perceptible against the stronger radiance of the lights below, flickered suddenly across the roof of the cave. The lie had turned into truth just as Barclay decided not to believe in it.

I flung my arm round Crispin's body, dragged him clean across me, and rolled over upon him as the gun went off. In the same moment I was aware of something that was launched from the rift above like a plunging bird, turning and twisting in mid-air with a dull yellow flash as it took the light. It struck Barclay's outstretched arm, and rebounded to clash against the rock below.

The bullet spat against the glazed stone not a yard from
my head, and whined in a series of squealing ricochets the
length of the gallery. I lay gasping and groaning over
Crispin's struggling body, my shattered hand doubled
helplessly under our combined weight, and couldn't lift
myself or turn to extricate myself from the scarifying pain.
But we were still alive, and that was a triumph so extravagant
that I could hardly believe in it.

Crispin wriggled from under me, and stooped to help me
with an arm under my shoulders. He was straining upwards,
panting with hope and excitement, towards the cleft in the
roof of the cave. The tongue of light was still there, hanging
motionless. On the ladder beneath it Barclay clung to the
quivering rungs, the pistol still in his hand. He was no
longer concerned with us. He stared wildly upwards, his
left arm braced firmly round the ladder, bringing the lance
of his lamp to bear upon the black hole above.

"Evelyn, did you see? Evelyn, there *is* somebody
there!" Crispin's arm contracted painfully round me, and
he lifted his voice to a frantic scream as the shape of a head
and shoulders leaned for an instant over the top of the
ladder, into the pencil of light. "Stavros, take care! He
still has the gun!"

Barclay flung up the pistol. The shot echoed and re-
echoed round the facets of the roof. The head was withdrawn abruptly, and the ladder creaked and tightened suddenly as though life had convulsed it. Somewhere aloft,
out of our sight, I felt what none of us could hear, the
grating protest of the staples straining in the rock. Barclay
gripped the rungs with frantic hands, and began to climb,
the great black box swinging clumsily behind him, com-
plicating balance and movement. Like a spider on a thread,
he scurried for the roof, the gun ready in his lifted hand.

The beam of lamp-light crossed the darkness and picked
out the pallor of a face, leaping from the upper air in

brilliant highlights and black shadows, a lean, muscular, vivid face with a hawk-like nose, staring down at us out of the black gallery beyond. There was less than ten feet between them when Barclay froze into stillness to take aim a second time.

Instead of stepping back from the rim, the stranger stooped and laid hold of the staples of the ladder. I saw only his black head, the curve of his shoulders arched in a great bow of effort. Crispin uttered a muted scream of anxiety and dread. Then the top of the ladder was heaved clear of the rock in one great explosion of energy, and Barclay, pistol, staples, lamp, treasure and ladder together sprang away from the roof and the wall, and crashed in a disintegration of metal and glass, almost at Crispin's feet.

The pistol flew spinning and slithering across the slimy floor. Crispin made a darting leap, and dropped upon it like a hunting leopard, springing back to my side and turning the muzzle upon his enemy as he waited for him to rise.

He did not rise. He lay on his back where he had fallen, arched horribly backwards over the steel box, his head dangling a thin ribbon of blood down the slope of the floor. His eyes were half closed. He was barely conscious, though little muttering, moaning breaths came from between his lips, and his body twitched for several minutes in long contortions that stiffened him to the finger-tips.

Crispin peered upwards in agonising doubt towards the distant face that leaned over from darkness into the ascending light, narrow and vivid as a flame. His hand clutched convulsively at the gun. " Stavros ? " he called in a quavering voice.

" Put that thing down ! " The voice echoed down to us threefold in a great hollow boom, rebounding from the faces of the rock. " You don't need it for me. Wait, I'll come down to you."

"Stavros, couldn't you go and telephone the police first ? And an ambulance ? Evelyn's badly hurt. And I think *he* is, too. He doesn't move, I think he's unconscious."

"So much the better," cried the voice grimly. "Don't touch him, don't go near him ! Don't let the gun out of your hand until I come. You're not afraid to be left with him ?"

"No, I'm not afraid. Do hurry, I'm frightened for Evelyn. When you come back, there are ropes and things in that box near the entrance."

"If he recovers enough to make trouble," ordered Stavros simply, "shoot him. You hear ?"

"Yes, Stavros."

All the tension of uncertainty ebbed out of his trembling legs, and his knees gave under him. He dropped to the rock floor beside me, took me by the shoulder, touched my hand, his lips quaking : "It's all right, Evelyn ! It's all right now ! Stavros Diakos—You know ? You remember ? He's going to get help for us. We'll get you safely out of here——"

He held on to me with one hand, and clutched the gun in the other, until the twitching body of his father's murderer became still. He didn't talk to me ; I think he was too far gone in exhaustion and reaction to have the energy to speak. But he kept close to me, and now and then he tightened his fingers very softly on my good hand, as though he were gently reminding me to stay alive. Those touches are all I remember of the next quarter of an hour.

Afterwards there were the two voices, and I knew Stavros was already with us. Lights moved about me, someone slackened the tourniquet, and sent live, blinding, grateful pain coursing down into my numbed arteries again, and brought me back for a few minutes to full consciousness. I saw an immensely tall, long-legged, narrow-flanked man soaring over me like an El Greco saint, elongated almost to the roof, and bending over me a craggy olive face. He had in his hand something that reflected back the light with thread-like golden gleams, and spread curved wings round from a thin, tapered centre-piece. Most things were hazy to me just then, but this was clear. I was looking at one—but which one?—of the twin frontlets from Pirithoön; and I knew, too, that this was what had come whirling out of the darkness above to deflect Barclay's aim with that first shot.

"Mine?" I heard Crispin ask, staring at the shining thing with enormous eyes, black with recollection.

"No. His," said Stavros. "I do not think it would ever have convicted him. But it does not matter now. His back is broken. The steel box broke it when he fell upon it. The gold of Pirithoön killed him."

"He isn't dead," whispered Crispin. "I saw him move only a minute ago."

"He will be," said Stavros with certainty, "before they come to fetch him." And suddenly he stalked across the rock floor to Barclay's side, and laid the frontlet over his soiled and distorted face. "Let him wear it—they were meant for the dead."

After that I sank back into the dark, and the rest of that night and the day that followed it remain blanks to me. They tell me I came round a couple of times while they were rigging gear and hauling me out of the cave, rolled in blankets and strapped to my stretcher like a dangling cocoon; but the police and a special rescue team were there by then, and they were experts at their job, and the operation was accomplished, so I'm told, with remarkable speed and neatness. Crispin says I swore like a trooper for the few seconds I was jolted into consciousness, but I fancy I'm being slandered. At any rate, they got me out somehow, and rushed me into hospital quickly enough to save both my life and my leg. I think Crispin stayed with me in the ambulance, but that part of it is pretty hazy.

I know Barclay wasn't with us. He was dead before they got to him, spread-eagled over his treasure-chest, wearing the death mask he himself had made. His skull was fractured, but from all accounts the spinal injury was the real cause of death. Stavros was right; it was the gold of Pirithoön that killed him.

CHAPTER XIX

THEY LET Dorothy in to see me on the third day, just for five minutes. She'd insisted on installing me in a private room, and filled the place with flowers, but until then I hadn't been allowed any visitors except the police. She brought me cigarettes and fruit, and sat by my bed looking beautiful and dazed, as though she had not yet grasped more than half of what had been going on round her.

" Crispin told me everything," she said, clinging to my hand. Told her everything? I very much doubted it. " Oh, Evelyn, how am I ever going to thank you ? "

" How is Crispin ? " I asked.

" Bruised and shocked, but he's going to be all right. He didn't feel the reaction so much at first, but next day he was really ill. Oh, Evelyn, I don't know whether I'm quite sane again yet ! The police got me up at six o'clock in the morning to tell me they'd fished you two and a dead man out of the caves. I thought it was some dreadful hoax. I was quite sure you were both in bed and asleep."

She trembled still at the thought, her hands quivering as she held mine tightly between them.

" 'Thank God Dermot was with you ! " I said.

" He's been a rock ! If you knew what hard work he

had even to make me understand what they were trying to tell me! I felt as though I'd been living on a volcano for months, and never known it until suddenly it blew up. That terrible man! I still can't grasp it. Even for all that gold—or all that glory——" She shut her eyes for an instant, and I knew she was seeing the hilltop in the Argolid, just as I'd seen it so often in my own mind. "He died. Did they tell you? There won't be any case. They opened the inquest this morning, but it's adjourned for a week now, they only took evidence of identification."

"I'm glad it isn't my job to find an acceptable formula," I said. "Self-incurred death in the course of committing a felony? Misadventure? It was certainly that! Lucky there are two sound witnesses to swear to the facts. Reasonably sound, at any rate! And what about the gold?"

"There isn't going to be any scandal, thank God! Dermot's arranging everything. He called the Greek Embassy, and went up to town to explain the whole case personally, and the authorities don't want to press any charges, they're only too staggered and delighted at such an unexpected windfall. So Crispin's got off lightly. But, oh, Evelyn, why didn't he tell me? Why didn't he ask me for help? I'd have done anything for him!"

"Crispin doesn't unload his responsibilities on to his womenfolk," I said disingenuously.

And then the nurse put her head in at the door and intimated with a silent stare that time was up, and Dorothy squeezed my unbandaged hand hard, and said we'd talk when I came home. It sounded a nice word, the way Dorothy said it. But my job at the Lawns was finished now. Bruce's murderer was known, and dead; Bruce's discoveries were safe; and so was his son.

Crispin came the next day. He looked exhausted, and rather blank, as though having his feud snatched out of his hands and resolved thus dramatically had left him at a loss what to do with his life and his energy. His face was still swollen and bruised, and he hadn't yet caught up on his sleep, for his eyes were hollow and blue-rimmed.

"Stavros is here with me," he said, "but they'll only let us in one at a time, and only for a few minutes each. Are you still as ill as that? I was hoping you'd soon be home. My mother's going to have you moved to the house as soon as the doctors will let you go. Evelyn, you are better, aren't you? Really better?"

I reassured him that I had the constitution of a horse, pints of other people's blood inside me, and every intention of being on my feet within another week.

"They made me go to bed for two days, too. There was nothing the matter with me, but I had to do as I was told. I was in enough trouble as it was. But in the end nothing whatever's happened to me, except a lot of lectures, and after Stavros the police were almost polite. I got a fearful telling-off from Stavros when he heard what I'd done. He said if I could sneak out of the villa after midnight to rifle the tomb, I could have sneaked down to the village while I was about it, and gone to him. And I suppose I could, I've often wished since that I had, only——" He averted his shadowed eyes, and looked bleakly into the past for a moment, into a time when he had been alone in the world, like Hamlet, with his father's ghost, and no one, not even Stavros, had been clean of the shadow of guilt.

"I don't think he'd hold it against you," I said, fumbling a cigarette with my plastered and bandaged hand, that had one broken metacarpus, and three fractures distributed among the finger-bones. He jumped to offer a light, eager to have something to do for me.

"And Dermot's undertaken to clear up the international mess I've made—did my mother tell you it's going to be all right? They're all wildly excited about the gold, it seems it's the most wonderful find for years. Pre-Trojan

War, they think, but they're still arguing about it. Bruce
will get his memorial, after all. He'll be Almond of Pirithoön, just as you said." It would matter desperately to
Crispin that Bruce's name should be bound up for ever
with that golden village in the Argolid, where he lay
buried. "They found our original mask, too. It was in
Barclay's baggage at the hotel."

"We seem to owe Dermot an apology, don't we ?" I said.
"Somehow I don't think your story can have surprised
him very much. We were right in concluding that he suspected you of having the stuff, but it looks rather as if his
object in coming here was not to rob you of your ill-gotten
gains, but to see the gold safely back to its owners with as
little damage as possible to you. Was that it ?"

"Yes. He says I left plenty of signs of my raid in the
tomb, even though my card was gone by the time he and
Stavros got there. Prints in the dust of hands and shoes
that indicated somebody my size—and who else was it
likely to be but me ? He kept it strictly to himself, even
from Stavros, because if I *had* plundered the tomb he
wanted the affair straightened out without a public rumpus.
That was why he wrote and invited himself to our place as
soon as he got back to England, and why he wanted to get
hold of me alone, only you wouldn't let him——"

"And why he searched your room ?"

"Yes, that was Dermot, too. It must have hurt his
uprightness quite a lot to have to do that, but he didn't
want to tackle me about it without being sure of his facts."

"So David was the only one who really turned up by
chance. It was quite a week-end party, wasn't it ?"

The pale smile warmed. "We'll have a better one when
you come home !"

He made it sound nice, too. It was strange how this
word "home" kept breaking in.

"Won't you be awfully tired ? Am I talking too long ?

an I send Stavros in for a few minutes ? Because he's
leaving in a day or two, he's going to London with the gold,
and as soon as the inquest's over he's going to take it back
to Greece. That's an honour, if you like ! But he deserves
it ! And he'd like to talk to you before he goes. About
me, I expect ! " said Crispin with a slightly distorted grin.
" He's probably going to warn you to keep a firm hand
on me."

" Send him in," I said, " I'd like to shake hands with
the only man who knows how to put you in your place."

He got as far as the door, and then came back in a rush
to fling his weight across my bed, shut his hands impulsively
upon my arm, and say warmly : " Evelyn——"

" Well ? Evelyn what ? "

" Nothing—just Evelyn ! I'm glad you're going to be all
right ! " His forelock brushed my sleeve. He picked himself up in a quick scramble, and whisked out of the room ;
and presently Stavros Diakos came in.

He looked less extremely tall and thin, indoors and in
full light ; just a long, rangy hill-man with a weather-
beaten face, and black eyes narrowed and sharpened by an
outdoor life in the brilliance of his native air. His movements about a sick-room were delicate and precise ; I could
hardly believe the same hands that placed his chair with
such considerate silence beside my bed had tried to tear
me apart only a few nights earlier.

We two already knew each other very well.

" I owe you two and eightpence and one drachma," I
said, " and a new coat."

" Also some bruises, I think," he said, in a countryman's
throaty bass, and his face creased into lines of good humour.

" And Crispin's life and mine," I said, and held out my
good hand. He took it, and the cuff slid back from his flat
brown wrist, and showed the small seam of his scar.

" I'm sorry if I hurt you the other night. I thought when

you pulled me from the wall that you were Barclay. He wa
there in the grounds, too, I followed him there."

"You followed him across Europe, didn't you?" I said.
"For Crispin's sake? Or Bruce's? And how did you know
it was Barclay? That's the one thing that's been puzzling
me all the time I've been lying here."

"You remember the mask, the one he sent back from
Athens? When we were clearing up at the site, after the
funeral, I found it among Mr. Almond's things in the
office, and I brought it to Crane, to ask what should be
done with it. He said at once that it was not the same one
he'd handled before. I thought about it for a long time,
and I reasoned that if he was right it must mean that the
original one had been stolen. And that meant that it had
a value we had not credited."

"In fact, you were thinking on the same lines as Crispin.
About the substitution, and about Bruce's death, too."

"About that, too. And Mr. Almond was my friend.
And I, too, reasoned that whoever had made the substitution would come back to the tomb—soon, as soon as
the site was deserted. I watched, and it was Barclay who
came back. One night his car was on the track below the
citadel, hidden from the village. I, too, found it incredible
that it should be Barclay, and I did not trust my own conclusion. So I thought it best to suggest to Crane that we
ought to go back and at least examine the tomb, to make
sure whether there was anything of value there. So much
we two could do alone. I wanted two of us, because some
day it might be a matter of giving evidence, and I needed
a witness."

"And the tomb," I said, "was empty. And all too plainly,
because of the bodies, it had not always been empty."

"There was still some pottery there, nothing more.
I knew, and Crane knew, that with those five dead there
must have been gold, and much gold. And I knew that

rclay had taken it away. I *thought* I knew it," he corrected mself, and smiled.

" Did you tell Crane what you believed, and what you'd seen ? "

" No. I was not on such close terms with him as I had been with Mr. Almond, and one hesitates to accuse an eminent man like Barclay of murder and robbery without proof. I wanted more before I shared my suspicions with anyone. I wanted the original mask. That was something no one would be able to explain away. So I asked Crane for a reference, and I applied for a job with Barclay in Athens. It was already being said that the Professor was completing his work there, and that he was taking back to England with him a great mass of material of a kind I was used to handling. My reputation is good among archæologists. I wished to be placed in charge of the packing and transporting of his cases. I told him it was my ambition to enter his service, and that was no lie. I did not tell him the reason," said Stavros, and his smile tightened suddenly into a stony coldness.

" So that's how you came to England ! Did you find the mask ? "

" I saw it, once, only once. He kept it always either on him or in his locked brief-case, but once I caught a glimpse of it as he took it from the case. It was wrapped in a scarf, but the covering slipped from one cheek-piece, and I knew it. Then I was sure that he was Bruce's murderer. The other mask, his, I carried always on me. It was of no value, Crane gave it to me when I asked for it. I wanted it as evidence when the time came, when I was able to lay my hands on the rest of the gold. I was sure he had it. I knew it had never passed through my hands, therefore he, and only he, must know where it was.

" After the cases were safely delivered here to the Museum I was paid off, with my fare back to Greece. But I did not go. I stayed in London, close to him, waiting for him to lead me to the gold. I had been one of his household, it was not difficult for me to get to know his movements. It was more difficult to understand them, especially when he led me here to this small town, and to Mr. Almond's house. I did not know whose house it was until I saw Crispin in that lighted room, and then I was so intent on him that I lost sight of Barclay. When you attacked me—well, it was natural to think first of my enemy. I hope I didn't hurt you ? "

" It was well worth it," I said, " to have you around in a crisis. I suppose you were following us last night, too ? "

" There was nothing else I could do. I did not know any longer what was happening, I did not know why he had come here, nor what he wanted with Crispin, but I knew that he was a murderer, and as dangerous to the son as to the father. I followed you all three up the hill, but on the hilltop I lost you. It is not hard to understand why. Crispin knew the entrance to the cave, and you, I think, made very sure that Barclay should find it. But I did not even know that there were caves there. If I had known, I should have kept nearer to my quarry. As it was, I hung back from you without any qualms on that open hillside. I saw you pass into the copse. Then there was no one in sight, no one in earshot. I spent all that time, while you and Crispin had so much need of me, casting about the hill from that copse, trying to pick up the trail again. From tree to tree, from rock to rock, and nothing."

I thought how easily he might have lost us for good, given up the hopeless chase and gone away, and left us to Barclay. " What saved us ? What led you to the entrance finally ? "

" The shot. The second shot, Crispin says—the one that blew the padlock off the box. I always came back, after

y false casts, to the copse and the rocks, and it so happened
nat I was close to the entrance when the shot was fired.
The echoes pass through that upper gallery very loudly
and clearly. The shot seemed to be fired right under my
feet. Then I knew you were there under the earth, and it
was only a matter of finding the shaft. When you know
what you are looking for, you have a better chance of
finding it."

"You found it in the nick of time for us," I said. "When
you threw the mask at him I believed in miracles. I still do.
We're alive, and you're going home in glory with the gold
of Pirithoön. Bruce's ghost must be well satisfied."

"He was my friend," said Stavros, "and a good man.
I'm glad he has his triumph, even after death. And the
boy is a good boy." He waited for me to speak, and I did
not speak. Nevertheless, Stavros smiled. "He will be safe
with you. I am well satisfied."

Safe with me. I lay thinking about that after he'd left
me, hunted out of the room by the nurse's reproachful face.
It seemed to me that there was no place left for me in
Crispin's life now. Both Dermot and David were absolved
from all suspicion of complicity in Bruce's death, and
Dorothy, who had not even known Barclay, was cleared
with them. Crispin would dwindle into a normal, cheerful,
gregarious adolescent, plunge head over heels into school
life, and fill the void left by his obsession with a hundred
diversified activities. He would hardly need me.

Or was there still one job to do before I bowed myself
out ? The removal of a minor shadow, but a persistent one.
There was still a certain letter to be accounted for.

"Dear D——"

I was removed to the Lawns after a week in hospital,
and though I travelled there in an ambulance, I was at
least allowed to walk to the ambulance on my own two feet,
for the bones of my leg were intact, and the wound was

mending remarkably well. The blood transfusions they'd spent a day and a half pumping into me hadn't been wasted.

That night, after dinner, which Dorothy brought to me in bed, Dermot came in to see me, at my request. When we'd disposed of all the loose ends, I asked him to go into Crispin's room, and bring me his copy of the Choephori. I shook the bookmark out of the book, unfolded it, and handed it to him.

"Please believe I have a good reason for asking about this. Do you recognise it ? Was it written to you ? "

He looked at it with tolerant surprise, and raised his eyebrows at me, but he answered patiently. Interesting invalids have their privileges.

"Yes, it was mine. Where did it come from ? "

"Dorothy wrote it ? "

He gave me a heavy stare, but after a moment assented coolly : "Yes."

"Were you corresponding regularly with her while you were in Pirithoön, and she was in Athens ? "

"Yes, I was. Any objection ? "

"Would you mind telling me about that correspondence ? It's of importance, or I wouldn't ask you."

"It was very simple," said Dermot. "Dorothy came to Greece because of Crispin. She'd held off as long as she could, but the truth is Dorothy was sick with wanting Crispin. I'd known her for some years, she trusted me, I knew how she felt. He was her boy, and she didn't even know him, and she was afraid he'd learned to think of her as an enemy. She came to Greece just to be near him, but she couldn't approach him directly. She felt she'd given him up too easily. She felt guilty about him. I used to send her news of him, snapshots sometimes." He flicked the slip of paper back on to the bed. " That's the ' he ' who wasn't to know that she was in Greece—Crispin himself. And the torn word, if you're interested in that, too, as 'reports,' as far as I remember. Reports about her on."

I felt oddly humiliated, as though I'd been the one to misjudge her. I thought of her lingering outside Crispin's door in the night, desperate for his affection, and my heart turned over with longing for her as hers must have been doing with longing for him.

"Will you forgive this last question, too ? " I asked. "Are you in love with her ? Even more particularly, is she——"

Dermot laughed. " No, nothing like that." He thought he understood everything now. " We're old friends, that's all. The field's all yours, old boy."

Nothing was more certain in my mind than that, even if there was a field, I didn't figure in it ; but I didn't feel it necessary to say so. Dorothy's anxiety and ardent kindness were all for Crispin's friend and ally, or perhaps a little for the boy who once lived next door and was like a brother to her, but not, I felt sure, for Evelyn Manville as a person and a possible husband.

" I wonder if you'd mind hunting up the brat," I said, " and telling him I want him."

Dermot sent him to me five minutes later. He came in balancing two glasses of sherry, and sat down on the side of my bed, and presented me with one of them. He hadn't quite lost the look of shock even yet, and I didn't think it was any reaction from his frightening experiences that had left that blankness in his face. I suppose it takes time to accustom yourself to going on living, and still longer to reorientate yourself to normality and the smallness of most human occasions, after dedicating your life voluntarily to a vengeance as certain to destroy the avenger as his enemy. He gave me a nice smile over the rim of his glass, and said : " Success to temperance ! "

I opened the Choephori on the quilt between us, without

saying anything, and unfolded the little strip of paper an
turned it towards him. The smile left his face. He grew
rather pale, and averted his eyes from mine to fix them on
the tiny thing that still shut out from him all peace of
mind.

"Where did you find it ? " I asked him gently.

In an almost inaudible voice he said : " Keeping someone's place in a book in the office at Pirithoön. Just after
I'd found the bogus mask. I didn't know who'd been
reading the book."

"But you knew the writing was your mother's ? "

"My father kept all her letters. I'd seen them too often
not to know the hand." " My father." He was back in
the ceremonial presence of justice, and Bruce's rights and
titles and injuries were all set forth in that dignified name.

"I see. And would you like to know exactly what this
letter means, and to whom it is written ? It was to Dermot.
And Dermot rightly felt so little guilt about it that he used
it as a bookmark, and left it in the office for anyone to find.
A little careless of him, seeing your mother had made a
point of secrecy ; but he regarded that as a hypersensitivity
on her part, you see. They were old friends, they'd known
each other for several years, and when Dermot went out to
Pirithoön with you and your father, your mother seized the
chance to ask him to send her news—of *you*."

The long lashes lay almost on his cheeks, and his face
was quite still.

"She came to Athens because it was as near as she
dared come to *you*. And she begged Dermot not to let
you know that she was there because she felt she had no
rights in you, and mustn't pursue or trouble you. What
made all the difference in the world to her was to know
that Dermot was there close to you, and that through him
she could get news of you regularly, pictures of you sometimes, a few crumbs, all she felt she had the right to ask

:. That's what her connection with Dermot meant to her. .nd that's why he was able to send for her immediately Bruce's death was discovered."

I reached out and took the sherry glass from him, and put it down on the table beside the bed, because his hand was shaking so that in another moment he would have dropped it. The directness of my attack had stripped every defence from him, I could feel his pitiful nakedness. He couldn't even pretend to himself or me that he had a secret any longer, I'd demonstrated my knowledge only too well, as though I'd laid bare his inmost heart and mind to the harsh daylight, and exposed there the long agony of his conviction of Dorothy's guilt.

" Crispin, I've known your mother since we were both kids. She never did an underhanded or cruel thing in her life, and she's an even poorer liar than you are. She was never unfaithful to Bruce once in all the years they were married—not even the time she said she was. That was a miscalculated piece of generosity on her part, and maybe she made an ass of herself. But who doesn't, sooner or later ? Even you, sometimes ! "

I'd hoped I could talk him gently round the corner of his crisis into calm water again, but the burden was too much for him. It was as though the months of his implacable, dedicated hostility to her lay quivering there between us, torn out of him by torture, like an effusion of blood, or a cry of pain. For the first time he saw it from the outside, as a nightmare, as a monstrosity, and sat helpless and sick with shame at having it exposed and knowing it unjustified.

His hands went up suddenly to his face, and through the tightly-closed eyelids and the compressing fingers his tears welled and spurted, first grudgingly, then in a shattering flood.

The decent thing would have been to look humanely in the opposite direction, and remember something I had to do somewhere else. Fortunately I was prevented from behaving like a gentleman by the fact that I was tucked firmly into bed, and so immobilised that tact would have been a monument of tactlessness. In any case, I was expendable. If he hated me for ever for being a witness of the flood I'd provoked, I could always remove myself from his sight and cease to offend; my job was over. So instead of pretending nothing out of the way was happening I hoisted myself up in bed and pulled him firmly into my arms.

He yielded to persuasion chiefly, I think, because he was past resisting ; but in a moment I felt him unclamp his hands from his face, and take firm hold of me by the pyjama jacket. Then his nose was buried in my shoulder, and his body softened and relaxed, abandoning itself thankfully into my arms in a perfect cloudburst of weeping. I patted his heaving shoulders, and poured a stream of nonsensical words into his one visible ear. At that stage the words didn't matter, anyhow, it was the tune that counted.

The Choephori slid off the bed, and closed with a plop over Orestes' monstrous predicament and Clytemnestra's death, over the appalling load of filial duty and the exclaiming chorus and the circling Furies. Crispin didn't notice the omen. Wildly grateful for deliverance from his suspicions, unbearably ashamed that he had ever felt them or I witnessed them, desperate to make amends for them, he clung to me and cried himself into a stupor of relief and exhaustion, dwindling in my arms until it was no longer an overwrought young man I held, but a disconsolate child waiting and ready to be comforted.

After a while, when the floods of tears had ceased to scorch and agonise, and the paralysing sobs no longer convulsed him, he detached one hand from its anchorage and began to grope blindly in his pockets. I gave him a large clean handkerchief, and he withdrew it into hiding with a

uffled gulp of thanks, and presently managed to croak out
f my shoulder, in a small, broken voice :

"Sorry, Evelyn—awfully sorry ! Bloody silly exhibi-
tion——"

"Now, now ! " I said. "That's enough of that
language ! "

"Oh, Evelyn, I'm so *ashamed* ! "

"Don't be silly, you've nothing in the world to be
ashamed of—only something to be glad about. What you
thought was very natural, but thank the lord it wasn't
true. And now it's all over, and we've all come out of it
safely. Now we can all make a fresh start. What is there
to cry about in that ? "

"Evelyn, you don't *know* what it's been like ! She was
so lovely—and so kind——"

"I know ! " I said. "You must always have wanted to
love her, and yet you felt you had to hate her."

He nodded vehemently, without raising his head.

"Well, now you can love her. There's nothing to stop
you any more. She loves you, you know. Very, very
much."

He whispered miserably, the tears gushing again : "She'll
loathe me when she knows what I believed about her——"

"She isn't going to know. Nobody in the world knows
but you and me, and after to-night we're going to forget
about it too."

"But, Evelyn," he protested wretchedly, "I shall have
to tell her everything. I've been so beastly to her. It
wouldn't be fair—she has the right to know——"

"You try it," I said smartly, "and see what you get !
Tell her everything, indeed ! What, unload the whole
thing on to her, just because it's too much for you ? No,
you've got to learn to live with your mistakes and failures,
the same as the rest of us. Even forgive yourself for them !
By the time you've made as many gaffes in your life as I

have in mine, you'll be quite good at forgiving yourself.
What are you worrying about ? You've got a lifetime to
make it up to your mother."

He sniffed, and said hopefully : " Yes, I have, haven't
I ? " By that time it was a more or less ordinary boy I
was holding. He sat up and dried his eyes, and blew his
nose hard. When I handed back his glass he gave me a
red-eyed grin over the rim as he raised it, and said : " All
right, here's to the future ! "

I kept him with me all the rest of the evening, since he
obviously didn't want to show his ravaged face downstairs.
We played a game of chess, which he won, and by the time
he said good night to me he was as clear and void as the
evening sky. After turning himself inside-out like that he'd
sleep as perhaps he'd never slept before, and wake up to a
world washed clean of everything that tormented and
reproached him, a virgin page ready to be written on.

At about eleven o'clock Dorothy tapped at my door, in a
velvet housecoat, with her dark hair loose on her shoulders.
Even on her way to bed she still walked with her head and
her elegant eyebrows raised, marvelling at a world which
was baffling to her, and opening her great eyes wide at the
complexities of human intercourse. It struck me that she
was going to find Crispin much less complicated than she
had hitherto found him to be, and that even his recoil into
innocence was going to puzzle her. Nobody can supply
fifteen years of mutual growth and experience to mother
and son who have been robbed of them.

" Listen, Dorothy ! " I said, inspired. " Do you know
what's been wrong between Crispin and you ? You're
afraid of him ! You've got it so firmly fixed in your head
that you did him an injury, that you approach him like a
beggar. It's very confusing for any boy. If it's difficult for
you to assert your rights in him, don't you think it's even
more difficult for him to assert his in you ? He may act

ke an adult at times, but he isn't one, and he isn't a child,
either, he's in the worst position of the lot, stuck between
the two. If you don't help him, he never will get to
you."

Dorothy said : " Evelyn, you know I'd do anything in
the world ! What ought I to do ? You're the only one who's
had any success with him, tell me what to do."

"'Easy ! You go straight into his room now," I said,
" just as you are, and put your arms round him and kiss
him. And not as if you were apologising for something,
either ! "

" Don't be silly ! " said Dorothy doubtfully. " He's been
in bed over an hour, he'll be fast asleep."

" So much the better ! Wake him up ! Truth will out,
if you startle him out of his beauty sleep."

She looked at me with a plaintive light in her eyes, and
a dubious sort of hope just curving her lips into a smile.
" Do you mean it ? Seriously ? "

" Never more serious in my life."

She must have been very desperate, or felt a desperate
faith in my judgment, because she went. When she came
back she was walking like one in a dream, and her fingers
were caressing her cheek, where his last penitent, adoring
kiss had rested, and her eyes had a look of dazed delight
that would have been funny if it hadn't been so touching.
She came and sat on my bed, and stared at me, and didn't
say a word.

" Well ? " I said, " was I right ? "

" Evelyn, how did you know ? Would it have been like
that if I'd done that the very first day ? Is that what he
wanted ? " Luckily she wasn't really looking for answers,
only enjoying the questions, and I didn't have to tell any
lies. " He opened his eyes, and smiled at me, and said :
' Mother ! ' and then put his arms up out of bed and hugged
me half to death. He looked such a lamb, Evelyn, all warm,

and soft, and flushed with sleep ! I've never been so happy ! "

" Don't expect him to be like that all the time," I said hastily. " And don't go imagining you've made some tragic mistake, the next time your lamb behaves like a normal little thug—just follow your maternal instinct, and box his ears, you won't be far wrong. And *he* won't question your judgment."

Dorothy patted my pillow into totally unnecessary tidiness, and smiled at me through a haze of happy tears. " Evelyn, you're—quite fond of Crispin, aren't you ? "

That was one question to which neither she nor anyone else was ever going to get a truthful answer. " He's not a bad kid," I said cautiously.

" He's awfully fond of you, Evelyn—he does need you still. You won't go away, will you ? He's a man's boy, he needs a man. I adore him, and maybe he does like me, too, maybe he'll learn to love me a little. But he needs a father——"

I hadn't had any premonition. Maybe she hadn't, either, until the word " father " slipped out to confront us both. She bent her head, and her hair drifted over me like black silk. Under its shadow I heard a soft, desperate laugh, watery with tears not far away. " Oh, Evelyn, it isn't only because of Crispin—but we could make a real job of taking care of him, between us. It's my turn this time : Evelyn, will you marry me ? "

" What, after the last fiasco ? " I said. But I didn't think at first that she'd even heard, much less recognised, the quotation, because I'd opened my arms, and she'd melted into them as naturally as if we'd both been twenty, and known each other only a few weeks, instead of all our lives. I couldn't believe it. This was how it ought to have been that first time, and couldn't be, because we had only a step to take into each other's arms, and from only a step away we saw each other out of focus. I kissed her cheek, and she turned on my shoulder to offer me her lips.

" It can't have been such a complete fiasco," she said, and I knew she was thinking of Crispin. " Will you, Evelyn ? "

" I'm broke," I said, " I haven't a job, but I love you, I always have, I always will. If the offer's open on those terms, I'll marry you joyfully, and straighten out the rest of the situation afterwards."

When she stirred and withdrew herself from my arms at last she patted tenderly at my pyjama jacket, and said softly : " I'm sorry, darling, I've left a wet patch on your shoulder."

It wasn't all hers, but I didn't tell her that. There are still things I don't tell her, even a few I hope she'll never find out. There isn't a grain of vanity in Dorothy, but after all, adorable though she is, she is a woman. She's already forgotten, in that convenient way women have, how mixed were her own motives for marrying me ; I wouldn't answer for her reactions if she ever suspects that I married her—well, *almost* as much for her son as for herself.